For my mother, Carol,
with whom I shared a love of mysteries
and who encouraged me to write one.

Blood Stained

A Madalyn Mitchell Mystery

*Tanya,
Enjoy your reading! —
Gayl Siegel*

Gayl Siegel

© 2022 by Gayl Siegel
All rights reserved. No part of this publication may be reproduced, distributed or transmitted in any form or by any means, including photocopying, recording, or other electronic or mechanical methods, without the prior written permission of the author, except in the case of brief quotations embodied in critical reviews and certain other noncommercial uses permitted by copyright law.

This is a work of fiction. Names, places, characters, and incidents are either the product of the author's imagination or are used fictitiously, and any resemblance to any actual persons, living or dead, organizations, events or locales is entirely coincidental.

Digital ISBN 979-8-9866475-0-0
Paperback ISBN 979-8-9866475-1-7

Cover design and illustrations by Kristina Helfert.

Printed in the United States of America

"And the Blood of Jesus Christ His Son cleanses us from all sin."

1 John 1:7

[NKJV]

CHAPTER ONE

Madalyn Mitchell gazed contentedly at the bright sunlight streaming through the stained-glass window. Small dust motes swam in the beams that alighted on the polished pew backs and spread across the church, finally alighting on the purple peony flower arrangements on the altar. The dust seemed to dance to the cadence of the sermon she was no longer really listening to. *Ahh,* she thought, *maybe Spring is finally here.* She was quite ready for Spring after another Iowa winter with heavy snow and single-digit temperatures. She soaked in the warmth as Jesus the Good Shepherd smiled down on her.

She had loved the stained-glass windows the first time she saw the pictures of the church that had been sent as part of the call package requesting that Rev. Jack Mitchell be the new pastor of St. Paul Lutheran Church in Marshallhaven, Iowa. The "call" was the word used for both the internal calling of God to the heart of a man to be a pastor, and also the external request from a congregation that a particular pastor come to shepherd their congregation. Hence, the "call package" was the collection of documents, including the formal request, the statistical and historical information about the congregation, and the salary and benefits that the congregation was able to offer as compensation for that shepherding, that the congregation sent out in hopes that the receiving pastor would accept.

Jack had accepted that call. That was ten years ago, and, despite the cold winters, they had been very happy here. They had moved around quite a bit, especially with moving to Fort Wayne, Indiana, where the seminary was, moving two years later for his one-year "internship", called a vicarage, at a congregation in Texas, and then moving back to seminary for his last year, only to turn around and move again to his first church in Arkansas. It was definitely different here in Iowa than in Texas or Arkansas, but Maddy hoped they would stay and retire here. She had friends here and it felt like home.

The church building itself looked like the quintessential hundred-year-old little white country church but had actually been built in the early 1980s. The previous church had been just such an old country church, but it had burned down in 1981, and the congregation wanted to rebuild in the same style. While keeping the white exterior, the steeple with the salvaged bell, and commissioning new stained-glass windows for both sides of the nave, they increased the overall size, added a parish hall and Sunday school rooms, and added niceties such as microphones, padded pews, and an electronic bell ringer—so that one need only push a button instead of pulling the heavy rope to ring the bell. They couldn't replace the altar, though. It had been one of the large, ceiling-high ornately carved altars with inset statues of Jesus and the evangelists. Alas, no one made such altars anymore, so they'd settled for a nice traditional, but ordinary, altar. To cover the back wall behind the altar, they'd purchased a huge crucifix with a nearly life-sized corpus. Frankly, it was the largest one Maddy had ever seen. She wondered if they'd had to go to a Catholic supply company to get it. It dominated the sanctuary and was even a little alarming on first sight. But by now she was used to it and liked it. It left no doubt in anyone's mind what this church was all about.

But the stained-glass windows were the pride and joy of the congregation. The original windows had been vibrant and detailed, showing ten scenes from the Old and New Testaments. It had never crossed anyone's mind not to replace them. She'd heard that the new ones depicted a few different scenes then the originals, but they were just as beautiful. Not that Maddy had seen the original windows. The rebuilding had taken place twenty years before she and Jack had moved there, but many of the congregation members had been here, remembered well, and were more than happy to expound at length on the tale of the sudden fire due to faulty wiring, the finding of another place to worship in the interim, the long year of rebuilding, and finally of the joyous dedication of the new church.

With a little start, she realized that the sermon was almost half over, and she hadn't heard a word. *Maybe the padded pews weren't such a good idea,* she thought wryly. The warm sunshine combined with a comfortable pew had certainly contributed to her woolgathering and nearly drifting off. They weren't entirely to blame, though. She knew the sermon practically word for word already, having heard it practiced on her twice yesterday, but that, too, was no excuse to daydream through it on Sunday morning. Being the guinea pig for Jack to practice on was an occupational hazard of being a pastor's wife. But there was a difference between listening for grammatical errors and awkward sentences on Saturday and hearing the Law and Gospel applied to her on Sunday.

She turned her attention back to the pulpit but was soon distracted again by the man standing in the pulpit. At 54, Jack had the good looks that are somewhere between 'distinguished' and 'rugged', and he was in reasonably good shape, due to Maddy's relentless efforts to get him to eat healthier and exercise every once in a while. Her efforts probably merely counteracted the beer and brats he indulged in at the various lunch meetings he attended, but she supposed everyone needed a treat now and then. His hair, completely grey, but still full and thick, looked good on him. Maddy herself was going grey, and much to her surprise, she found the intermingling of silver with her dark, nearly black hair attractive. It tended to accentuate her green eyes. She was glad she'd decided not to color her hair when she found the first strands of grey in her late thirties. She was also determined to not give in to the prevailing trend of middle-aged women cutting their hair very short and gelling it into stiff curls. She kept her hair full and wavy, just about shoulder length. Not that the short styles didn't look nice on her friends, it just wasn't her. Overall, having just turned 50 last year, she was enjoying life.

She and Jack had more time together now that their youngest of three, Mark, had started college last Fall at the University of Iowa. He still didn't know what he wanted to major in, but he had time to decide. After having two girls two years apart early on in their marriage, they had waited for eight years to have another child. At some indefinable point, they had come to the conclusion that more children were unlikely, and they had adopted Mark, a five-year-old boy from China. Despite the fact that he was only three years younger than Joanna, the two older girls always thought of him as their baby brother.

Martha and Joanna both knew early on what they wanted to do in life. Martha was now a Lutheran school teacher in Indiana, married to a pastor, with a baby on the way, and Joanna was getting a master's degree in some kind of physics (*astrophysics? quantum physics? something like that*) at MIT. It was a good thing she'd gotten scholarships, because they never could have afforded such an education on a pastor's salary. Joanna looked like Maddy, with black smooth hair but with rich brown eyes rather than green, while Martha took after Jack, with his square chin and almond shaped eyes. Martha's curly brown hair was starting to go grey early as well, despite being only twenty-four years old. She was starting to think about dying it. So many young women did. To each her own.

Jack's intensely blue eyes gazed out at the congregation, making eye contact with first one, then another—a maneuver that convinced each parishioner that he was speaking to them and only them. She noticed that Jack's hair was due for a haircut and was starting to curl a little behind his ear. She loved that little hint of a curl at his neckline. It made her want to reach up and twirl…

And then Jack was saying "Now may the peace of God keep your hearts and minds…". Oh, good grief, the sermon was over, and she hadn't heard a word. She quickly picked up her hymnal and started turning to the right page so it wouldn't be so obvious she'd been woolgathering during the sermon. *Thank goodness for a regular liturgy,* she thought sheepishly as she started singing "Create in me a clean heart, O God" from memory.

The sun had shifted and colored light from the windows was warming her again as she stood in line for communion. This time it was shining through the window depicting Noah's ark on the other side of the nave. *Now that was an old word,* she thought. The word 'nave' had the same root as the words 'Navy' and 'naval', meaning ship. The church had been referred to as a ship since ancient times, symbolizing the carrying of its passengers in safety over a dangerous ocean to a safe harbor, as the ark had carried Noah and his family safely through the flood. The church was a place of safety amidst the tumult of the world, carrying the faithful to heaven. Many people mistakenly referred to the church as a sanctuary, but technically the sanctuary was the portion of the church up front where the sacred things were—the altar and the elements of the Lord's Supper. The word 'nave' definitely carried a connotation of safety. With the sun warming her here in the church, Maddy did feel safe. Safe in the church, in her home, in her town, in her life. The warm sunshine made her think of Spring again. She should be able to plant her garden soon, after Easter when things settled down a bit. Being married to a pastor meant that the six weeks of Lent, culminating in Easter, were hectic and most projects got postponed until after Easter.

She looked again at the window, and her eyes focused on a shape in amongst the animals on the ark. It looked just like a spray bottle. Her hazel eyes focused sharply as she stared in disbelief. She blinked a couple times, looked away for a moment, and looked back. It still looked like a spray bottle. An ordinary every day, but definitely modern, spray bottle. What was a spray bottle doing in an Old Testament scene? Someone tapped her on the shoulder. Everyone in front of her had moved up to the communion rail and she was holding up the rest of the line. Her face burning with embarrassment, she joined the others at the rail and knelt. She was really going to have to pay more attention in church. Funny how the more one tried to keep focused, the more one's mind wandered. She offered up a quick prayer, "Lord, please help me keep my mind on the service and not embarrass myself anymore!" With firm resolve, she did not even look at the window for the rest of the service.

As she filed out at the end of service, she chatted casually with those around her.

"So, are you planting a garden this year?" asked Sandra Carlisle.

As she turned to answer, she snuck a quick peek and saw that without the bright sunlight shining through it, the colors were darker and the spot she'd noticed before didn't really look like a spray bottle anymore. She could see that it actually was part of two different animals next to each other. She remembered hearing things like someone claiming to see the face of Satan in the smoke of the burning Twin Towers on 9-11, and someone else making the news by finding a Cheeto that looked like Jesus. Not unlike the game of finding pictures in the clouds, her mind had found a picture of a spray bottle in the jumble of colors and lines of the stained-glass.

Relieved that she wasn't going nuts, she replied, "Yes, but maybe not as big as last year. Tomatoes, of course, and some of the other staples. No zucchini, though." She grimaced as Sandra laughed. Last year her zucchini had grown so fast they'd become huge before she could get them in. She'd brought box after box to the Garden Spot—the table set up in the parish hall where people could share the extras from their gardens.

"Don't feel bad," said Sandra. The two of them took synchronized infinitesimal steps toward the back of the church where Jack was shaking hands with and greeting the parishioners. "The same thing happened to me the first year I planted zucchini. You wouldn't believe the recipes I came up with to use it up. Zucchini bread, zucchini soufflé, zucchini casserole, stir-fried zucchini, zucchini cakes. I fed so much of it to Dad, he said he would turn green!"

Maddy joined in her laughter now. Sandra's father, Lenny, was a real card, always joking. His jokes weren't exactly original nor terribly witty, but he was fun to be around and always lightened the mood, whether the occasion was a church workday to clean the building and grounds, or the annual picnic.

Sandra was fun-loving, like her father, and attractive. Maddy wondered again as she had before why she'd never married. Although, the prospects in Marshallhaven weren't exactly great. The town was a decent size for a rural town, but all the marriageable young men went to the cities after high school and college. That was where the jobs and careers were. She approached the back of the church and smiled as Jack pulled her close and gave her a peck on the cheek.

"Hey, Pastor," said Lenny loudly from behind her, "How come the other ladies don't get a kiss?" It was a running joke, and Jack laughed. "She won the prize for being the one hundredth worshiper today!" he replied.

"Well, I just hope I don't ever win that prize! No offense, Pastor." Lenny grimaced in mock horror at the thought, and the other worshipers joined in the laughter.

Chapter Two

Maddy was still smiling as she headed across the parking lot to the parsonage. The parsonage had not been built by the congregation but was one of a string of similar houses built in the late 1960's in a 3-4 block area near the church.

The congregation had purchased the one on the corner just across from the church parking lot when they had called a pastor with a family. The congregation's first pastor had been a bachelor who was happy to live in a small apartment a few blocks away. He'd lived to a ripe old age and finally retired, and the next pastor had a family with four children. That was eight pastors ago, and the parsonage had been in constant use since then. So many churches had sold their parsonages or converted them to youth activity and office space that one only found parsonages in their original intended use in rural congregations these days. It was a white four-bedroom ranch style with a full basement and a large picture window in the living room. Maddy loved the large, farmhouse-style kitchen, perfect for cooking and baking for a family of five. Now it was a bit big for just the two of them, but it was home.

Upon entering the front door, she kicked off her shoes and nudged them in amongst the rest of the motley collection of boots and shoes next to the door. She padded into the kitchen in her stocking feet to start a fresh pot of coffee. Although she and Jack almost always drank decaf, on Sunday mornings he wanted the fully caffeinated variety, served black, and plenty of it. She noticed that there was less than a cup left and poured it down the drain. After rinsing the carafe and starting a pot of decaf, she started some soup warming on the stove and sliced some homemade bread. Then she sat down at the table, pulling a half-finished book of Sudoku puzzles toward her and started working on the next puzzle. Allegro, the smaller of their two cats, immediately jumped in her lap and made herself comfortable. Mark had named the cats Andante and Allegro. He'd always loved music—playing piano, singing in the children's choir—and she'd often thought that if there were better career opportunities in the world of music education he might pursue it more. Sadly, so few schools had music programs anymore. One had to be not merely good, but exceptional to make a career of music. He was also good at math. Maybe he would decide on a career in mathematics or engineering.

She glanced at the little cuckoo clock as it chirped twelve times for noon. Jack could be home in twenty minutes or two hours. It all depended on who wanted to talk to him after service. It didn't matter that he had open office hours during the week, mostly spent in utter solitude; most people felt more comfortable buttonholing him after church on Sunday. Oh, well. Sunday evening was their together time. They usually watched a movie and ate popcorn and pizza. Monday was his day off—on paper, anyway. At least he got to sleep in most Mondays, but unless they actually left town, work always seemed to intervene during the day. At least the church council had stopped scheduling meetings on Mondays. It was an improvement. Thinking of pizza, she checked on the pizza dough in the fridge. It was fully thawed and rising nicely and would be ready for toppings in a few hours.

She turned her attention back to her puzzle. Puzzles relaxed her, yet helped her mind feel more alert.

Two cups of coffee later, with cream and hazelnut syrup and plenty of sugar, Maddy realized that an hour and a half had gone by and Jack still wasn't home. Allegro was still napping contentedly in her lap, but her left leg was starting to go to sleep, so she carefully picked up the little calico cat and moved her to a nearby chair. Allegro just adjusted herself and went back to sleep. Maddy got up to stretch, looked out the window and saw Jack walking wearily across the church parking lot. She checked the soup to make sure it hadn't burned on the bottom, warmed the bread in the microwave, and poured a fresh cup of coffee. He opened the door, took off his shoes, plopped his briefcase on the hall table and turned to give Maddy a big kiss.

"Mmmm. It's good to be a Lutheran," he said, and smiled. It was his running joke that started when he'd made friends with Father Patrick, the Catholic priest, who'd remarked that although they both wore clerical collars, there were distinct differences between them. It was also good for a laugh at the town ministerial meetings where Tom Baker, the Baptist pastor, resolutely ordered ginger ale as the rest of them enjoyed a beer with their lunches.

"What kept you? That is, if it's something you can talk about," she asked as she dished up two bowls of steaming hot Minestrone soup.

"Oh, it's nothing private. Actually, Joe wanted to talk to Stan and me." Stan Johnson was the congregation president, and Joe Buchholz was the county sheriff.

"Is something wrong?" she asked.

"Well, no, not anything to do with the church. Hmmm. Well, sort of. Uh, I'm not making any sense. Let me start over." He took a breath. "The body of an unidentified man was found in the park down by the river. Although there was nothing on him to readily identify him, he did have our bulletin from last Sunday in his pocket. Joe thought he might be one of our parishioners, but neither of us recognized him from the photo. They're checking with the state missing persons log and hopefully they'll be able to use fingerprints and dental records to identify him, but in the meantime, they'd like us to keep our ears open for anyone who might know or be connected to this apparently new arrival in town. Maybe someone will report him missing in the next couple days. The big thing is that he was obviously murdered. Strangled—with a belt or something. So, yes, something's wrong, but no, not anything that involves us. He could have picked up the bulletin anywhere. Lots of people take them home, and then toss them when they're out having lunch, or use them as scrap paper. He certainly didn't get it at service last Sunday. We didn't have any visitors last Sunday."

That's not surprising, Maddy thought to herself. She blew on a spoonful of soup to cool it while she reflected on church attendance dynamics. They usually didn't have visitors. The town was small, and the demographics were definitely aging as the young people moved to the cities and family size decreased. Some people were worried that the church wasn't growing very quickly, but, although the congregation was aging along with the town population, they actually had a fair number of young families with children. That seemed to be the only set that was moving out to the smaller towns—young families that wanted to raise their children outside the rat race in the cities. Some worked for the few businesses in town or started their own small businesses, some were artists and craftsmen that traveled around to fairs and shows, and some were able to telecommute most days and make the 45-minute commute to Des Moines only once or twice a week. One young father was a medical transcriptionist for Mercy Hospital in Des Moines and worked out of his home. But despite these valiant souls determined to find a slower paced life, the majority of people who wanted more than a job stocking shelves at the local big box store had to move to where the jobs were. Oh, well. The town was still a nice place for people to retire. Quiet and small-townish, but close enough to Des Moines to have access the amenities of a city.

She looked at the clock again. "That didn't take an hour and a half did it?" she asked suddenly.

"Um, no. Harold Broomfield wanted to talk to me, too."

Maddy groaned. "What did he want this time?" she asked.

"He wanted me to stroll around the chancel while delivering my sermons and not, as he put it, 'woodenly read my sermon while being surgically attached to the pulpit.'"

"Your sermons aren't wooden!" exclaimed Maddy loyally.

"That's not the real issue. It's a matter of control. He wants to make changes that will result in a more 'dynamic' worship service that will 'attract young people,'" Jack said with a smirk. He broke a piece of bread, dipped it into his soup, and took a bite before continuing. "I told him that the pulpit was good enough for Martin Luther and C. F. W. Walther, so it was good enough for me. I also said that I'd probably trip or lose my train of thought if I pranced around the chancel. Although that might make worship more interesting. No, my style is my style and I'm not changing it."

"I'll bet he wasn't happy about that," mused Maddy. She laughed to herself at the image of a hoard of young adults standing outside the church, tapping their feet, saying 'if only he wouldn't deliver his sermons from the pulpit, we'd be right in there!' Harold had been trying periodically for years to make contemporary changes to the church. He seemed to think that catering to the culture would somehow conjure up a bunch of youthful new members and the church would grow into a mega church like Willow Creek or Saddleback. Not only were such tactics in direct conflict with Lutheran doctrine and practice, but there simply wasn't a large youthful population in Marshallhaven to draw on. At one church council meeting, Harold had loudly declared that there weren't enough babies and children in the church and that the pastor wasn't doing enough about it. Jack had raised an eyebrow and asked him in an amused and suggestive tone how exactly he was supposed to produce more children in the congregation. Everyone had laughed except Harold, who had dropped that particular angle. But if it wasn't a demand for contemporary music or more dynamic preaching, it was for programs and 'small groups.'

Maddy quietly got up and dished more minestrone into Jack's bowl.

"Thanks! How did you know I wanted more?" he asked in mock surprise.

"Well, maybe it was the wistful look on your face as you started scraping the bottom of the bowl with your spoon. I was afraid you might start licking it clean." She smiled and pushed the plate with the last piece of bread toward him. She started cleaning up while Jack finished his soup.

"So, do you think Elmer was too upset at me this morning?" She resolutely kept her back to Jack, waiting for his answer.

Jack sighed. "I know you mean well, but maybe you shouldn't say everything that comes into your head during Bible class."

"But he said that we should practice open communion! It's so frustrating! He keeps bringing up that the reason he joined the church was because the pastor who was here twenty-five years ago let him commune even though he wasn't Lutheran, and others would join, too, if we weren't so 'rigid'!"

"Do you think I agree with him?" Jack carefully opined, "or do you think I won't teach the rest of the class, or the congregation, that the practice of closed communion is both loving and Biblical?"

"No." Maddy calmed herself and turned. "I'm sorry. It's not my job to correct doctrinal errors. It's yours."

Jack smiled, slipped his hand into hers and pulled her closer. "I know you mean well. 'Nuff said?" Maddy nodded sheepishly and changed the subject.

"So, what movie shall we watch tonight? I got a couple more from Netflix yesterday. One's called *Breach*, a true story about that spy, Robert Hanssen, that they caught several years ago, and the other is the latest in the Narnia movies, *The Voyage of the Dawn Treader*."

"Well, let's take a look." Jack put an arm around her waist as they moved into the living room.

Later that evening, they were snuggled up on the couch, each with a lap cat, watching the end of *Breach* as Robert Hanssen was handcuffed and placed in the FBI van. The two main characters who had worked to expose Hanssen's treason were asking soberly what made a person decide to betray their country.

Maddy suddenly remembered the murdered man and thought to herself, *What makes a person decide to commit murder?* A chill went down her spine. It seemed somehow unreal. This was Marshallhaven. Small town, friendly community. It wasn't just that murders didn't happen here, which they didn't, but the idea of one person deciding to kill another in cold blood that really bothered her. Even in the heat of passion, Maddy couldn't conceive of wishing someone dead. She sighed and told Jack what she was thinking.

"Don't worry too much about it," he said, and gave her a kiss on the forehead. Joe and his deputies will find the killer," he said. He ejected the disc and turned off the DVD player and TV. Maddy picked up the empty popcorn bowl and used napkins. There was one piece of pizza left, but Jack had picked off the pepperoni and mushrooms. She tossed it into the bowl with the used napkins to be discarded and sighed. Jack was right that she shouldn't dwell on it, but she still felt kind of queasy. Was she being naïve? She knew murders happened all the time, in other places. But she thought of all the people she knew and was sure that not one of them was capable of deliberately ending the life of another. She finished cleaning up and joined Jack in bed. Snuggling up next to him made her feel safe and she went to sleep.

CHAPTER THREE

Maddy felt trim and attractive in her beige linen pantsuit as she pushed open the heavy glass door of the community health center and waved to her friend Penny, who was sitting behind a gunmetal gray utilitarian desk with a slightly out-of-date PC, and stacks of papers on the desktop. Penny got up from her desk, shrugged on her pale green cardigan, grabbed her purse and headed towards her across the bare tile floor.

"I'm glad you're a little early" she said "lunch might be a little short. I have to be back right at one for a meeting with the mayor."

Penelope Olson was a public health nurse with the county health department, and the Spring Health Fair was coming up. Mayor Horace Weatherby loved being involved in civic events, which meant a little micromanaging and a lot of support from the city.

She, too, was in her early fifties, but projected a youthful image with her jet-black dyed hair chopped short and gelled into a spiky halo. She also usually wore red nail polish, red lipstick, and large hoop earrings. Maddy often wondered how she pulled it off without looking ridiculous, but she projected an aura of youth, vigor and enthusiasm. It was a persona that had stood her in good stead as a public health nurse, who is often the bearer of unpopular news. ...*I'm sorry, but I'm going to have to close your restaurant until you correct these deficiencies.... Yes, you need to have a doctor clear your child once he recovers from Hand, Foot and Mouth disease before going back to school. ... Because you handled the bat you caught in your bedroom, you'll need to get four rabies shots over the next four weeks. ... No, you can't sell hot dogs from a sidewalk cart without a permit and a foodhandler's license.* Yet somehow, Penny was able to deliver these messages with a mixture of concern and authority that got people to comply.

Penny had never married, but she had been engaged. After getting her three-year nursing degree from Concordia College in River Forest, Illinois, she had returned to her home town and begun working at the nursing home. Robert had come into her life in 1989. In his second year of dental school, he'd come to Marshallhaven to discuss joining the dental practice of his grandfather, Old Doc Reinhart, once he graduated. He spent the summer working for his grandfather as a receptionist/assistant and made up his Army National Guard drill and training days that he had missed while in dental school at Camp Dodge in Des Moines. They had fallen in love and he had come back the next summer to work out the final details with his grandfather and complete more national guard training days.

By July of 1990 Bob and Penny were seriously talking about their future together, but in August his unit was called up for Operation Desert Shield. She was proud of him answering his country's call. He got a one year deferment from dental school and packed his bags. He gave Penny an engagement ring and promised that they would get married as soon as he returned. She kissed him goodbye, and never saw him again. They wrote to each other several times a week, and just before Christmas, he wrote saying that he would be staying longer than expected.

The letters continued and their love deepened with the separation. But four months later Desert Shield has become Desert Storm, Iraq had been pushed back out of Kuwait, and Bob had been killed by a sniper. She spent a whole day crying in her mother's arms, then she dried her tears and went to his funeral. She wore his engagement ring for a year, and on the anniversary of his funeral, she placed it in a velvet-lined box that sat next to his photograph. She got on with her life, got a well-paying job with the county health department with benefits and pension plan, and took care of her father after her mother died. Although she had dated a few men, she never loved anyone like she had loved Bob.

Penny had told Maddy all this soon after they'd met, and they had become fast friends. Maddy had looked sadly at the photo of the handsome young man in his Army uniform.

"He's waiting for you in heaven, you know," she said.

"I know," said Penny simply.

Maddy had wondered how she would handle it if she lost Jack. The thought terrified her, and she didn't think about it if she could help it.

"So what's the theme this year?" asked Maddy. She always enjoyed the health fair and usually volunteered to take blood pressures. She herself had finished nursing school, had gotten her RN license, and practiced for six months when she and Jack were first married. But when she found out she was pregnant with Martha, she'd quit and become a full time homemaker and mother. She'd never regretted the decision and had loved being home with her children and husband, but she liked to keep a connection with the medical world.

"Food Borne Illness," answered Penny, with a little smile. Maddy looked surprised.

"Food poisoning? Really?" Maddy looked thoughtful for a minute. "I was about to say I couldn't think of any outbreaks, but then I remembered the huge recall on eggs a couple years ago from that farm right here in Iowa, and the spinach and lettuce recalls the year after that."

Penny was nodding. "Recalls for contaminated food products are on the rise. And with food being distributed more widely, outbreaks aren't the localized affairs that we used to see in the past, but more spread out. In addition, people still tend to have poor food practices in the home and especially during the summer picnic season when potentially hazardous foods can sit out at warm temperatures for several hours. There's plenty of material for education. In fact, we probably should have done this theme a long time ago."

"Well, let me know how I can help out," she said as they walked across the street to Sarah's Bakery. Sarah Anderson was a self-made woman. She'd started the bakery almost twenty-five years ago, and now it was a fixture in the town as a lunch haven for those who worked downtown, a dispenser of doughnuts and pastries for kids after school, and the undisputed source for cookies or rolls for whatever family or civic gathering one might be organizing. At Christmastime she outdid herself with pies, lefse, pfefferneuse, and an unlimited supply of melt-in-your-mouth painstakingly decorated sugar cookies. It was a either a foodie's dream or a dieter's nightmare, depending on your point of view. Maddy breathed in the delicious smell of baking bread as she took a seat at their usual table near the back wall of the clean, cozy dining area. She pushed her purse under her seat, smoothed the green gingham tablecloth, and hitched her chair up to the table.

"Did you hear about the body they found in the park?" she asked as she reached for the basket of assorted rolls that the waitress always placed on the table before taking their order.

"What? A body? Like, a *dead* body?" said Penny in surprise.

"Mmm-hmmm." She swallowed her bite of caraway rye before continuing. "A stranger in town, apparently. They're trying to identify him. I guess he had one of our Sunday bulletins on him, but neither Jack nor Stan recognized his photo."

She paused and glanced up. "Oh, Sorry," she said to the waitress, who was waiting next to the table and listening with interest. "I'll have a turkey club with extra mustard on sourdough, and a raspberry lemonade." Penny ordered a Ruben on marbled rye bread, water with lemon and without ice, and a lemon bar, then turned back to their conversation.

"So, what, he died of exposure? Or a drug overdose or something?"

"Hmmm? Oh, no, I'm sorry I should have said; he was murdered—strangled." The waitress had moved to the next table, but was still obviously trying to catch the conversation. She finished taking the order of the couple next to them and sidled toward the kitchen, still trying to hear what Penny and Maddy were saying.

Penny gaped at her "Murdered? Murders don't happen here. This is Marshallhaven. I mean, in Des Moines or the Quad Cities, sure, but not here!"

"I know," said Maddy, "We have petty crime, vandalism, hooliganism, but not murder. Well, I guess there was that time a couple years ago when that woman was stabbed by her live-in boyfriend, but she survived, so I guess that was attempted murder. Still, violent crime just doesn't happen here. Most people don't lock their houses or cars and they don't have to worry about their kids walking alone to the city pool in the summertime. I guess it just goes to show that human nature is the same everywhere."

Their sandwiches arrived quickly, and the waitress hovered, hoping for more salacious news. Penny smiled and asked, "You're Donna's niece, aren't you?"

"Yes, Ma'am," said the girl shyly. She looked to be about 17 or 18, with wispy straight blond hair that fell into her eyes.

"I remember you from last summer when you came to your grandmother's funeral. You're from Adel, right?" The girl smiled, pleased to have been remembered, but didn't volunteer any more information.

"I'm Penny and this is Maddy. What's your name?" Penny asked. "Amy" was the succinct reply. "Um, I'd better get back to work…" she added, her voice trailing away at the end.

"Of course. Nice to meet you!" said Penny brightly as the girl ducked her head and shuffled back to the kitchen.

Penny turned back to Maddy and steered the conversation elsewhere. "So, what else have you been up to?" she asked.

"Oh, you know, I've got three soap operas to keep up with." said Maddy airily. Penny laughed. They both knew that Maddy worked as hard as most women who worked outside the home. With no time clock, Maddy tended to take the attitude of 'Why buy it when you can make it?' She sewed clothes for her family, baked bread, and made everything from mayonnaise to yogurt. In addition, she tended to take on projects, volunteer at church and in the community. She used to be surprised at the end of a 12- to 16- hour day and wonder where the day had gone. But now she actually wasn't as busy as she used to be. With Mark off to college, she sometimes found that she did have extra time now and then. She missed the cheery chaos of having kids around, her kids and their friends, slamming the front door, or eating an entire batch of cookies before they made it to the cookie jar, watching a movie sprawled all over the living room. Still, she had plenty to do. A lot of what Maddy did was to help make Jack's life a little easier and make sure he ate and slept occasionally. Few people realized how much work a pastor puts in every week. Between Sunday services, writing sermons, Wednesday Bible class, confirmation, visiting shut-ins, youth group, men's group, family night, vacation bible school, and special holiday services during Lent and Advent, he worked about seventy to eighty hours per week. Being a pastor's wife was a job she loved, knowing that her efforts were well appreciated. When Jack had started seminary, they had both met with the advisor. Most of the questions were directed at Jack, asking about his background and why he wanted to become a pastor. Maddy was startled when the advisor had turned to her with a little twinkle in his eye and asked, "So, are you ready to become a Pastor's wife?" It was then that she had the first inkling that being a Pastor's wife was more than just being married to a Pastor.

"So do you think they'll bring it up at the community meeting on Thursday?" Penny was asking.

"What?" said Maddy.

"The murder, of course. I think having someone strangled in the park is definitely of interest to the community." Once a month, there was a community meeting at the town hall, with updates on pertinent issues by the mayor, chamber of commerce, fire chief, county sheriff, police chief and sometimes civic organizations like the Lions and the Kiwanis.

"Well, if they don't volunteer anything, you can certainly ask. It's bound to be in the paper this week and I'm sure lots of people will want to know if there's a crazed serial strangler on the loose in town."

"Well," Penny said seriously "One murder hardly qualifies as a 'serial strangler' but it is of concern. Oops, it's almost one. Gotta go." She laid a few bills on the table, picked up her purse and headed out.

"See you Thursday!" she called, and she was gone.

Maddy slowly pulled two five-dollar bills from her wallet. Could it be a serial killer? Would there be more killings? If she thought about it logically, there were only a few possibilities. Either it was a stranger killing or it was done by someone known to the victim. If the first, then the motive could be something like robbery or possibly someone crazed with hatred of a particular class, race, or other group, like vagrants. Not very likely because he seemed to be a stranger in town with not much worth stealing and he was a white man, so a racist or sexist hate crime didn't seem to fit. Unless he was gay, but there was no way to tell that if he was a stranger in town. On the other hand, if he was a stranger in town, and no one knew him, then no one in town had a motive. The second alternative, in which the motive would then be personal to both the murderer and the victim, would mean that he wasn't a stranger to someone in town. Perhaps someone who was pretending to not know him. Even though he was apparently a stranger in town, the second possibility seemed much more likely. Random violence was virtually unknown here and it was more likely that he was known to somebody or more than one somebody in town. Why else would he show up here at all? It's not like there were jobs to draw someone. He must have come to see someone who lived here. But to even begin to discover the motive they would have to identify the victim, which the police were already working on, and then find out what connections they might have to anyone in the community.

Maddy realized she'd been frozen with two five-dollar bills in her hand suspended over the table for several minutes. She placed them on the table, picked up her purse, waved to the waitress, and headed for home.

CHAPTER FOUR

Jack and Maddy smiled and greeted those around them as they made their way into the crowded town hall. The town hall was the old National Guard Armory, no longer used as such, which consisted of a large open space with a small, minimally equipped kitchenette at the back where coffee and trays of Sarah's cookies were laid out. The din of voices swelled comfortably around them echoing off the bare walls and metal folding chairs. There wasn't always this crowd of people. Some months saw only a handful of people matching the sparse agenda, but tonight's meeting was of particular interest to the community because the Spring snow melt was underway and flooding was a yearly issue.

Sure enough, representatives from the Army Corps of Engineers were passing out graphs of projected flood levels and setting up power point slides to address the issues associated with the dam upriver and the levy on the northwest side of town. Both were a few decades old now, and many were concerned about the potential failure of one or both. The mayor would talk about the sewer issues and rerouting traffic if some of the streets near the river flooded. Fortunately, most years did not see flooding in the streets, but many years saw flooded basements and, every seven to ten years, heavy rainfall combined with rapid melting of the heavy snowpack upriver in Minnesota would result in considerable losses to homes and vehicles. There had been several flood mitigation efforts in the past such as sewer backflow prevention and shoring up of the levy, but the town, like so many others was built right on the river and flooding was inevitable. About twenty years ago after the last really huge flood, the homes right down on the river had been demolished and the land turned into a park, the same park where the stranger had been strangled.

They sat down next to Stan and Janet Johnson. Stan was gently seating Janet in her chair before he sat down. He was a surprisingly gentle man for his size and build. He was a good 6'2" and had the stocky muscular build of a man who had spent most of his fifty-odd years working on the farm. His hands were twice the size of Janet's, and his left hand completely engulfed her right one as they sat hand in hand. It was so sweet the way he took care of her. He had lost his first wife to ovarian cancer when she was only twenty. They'd been married only a year when she died, and he had been devastated. This of course was long before Jack and Maddy had moved to Marshallhaven, but she'd been filled in by Penny. Maybe it explained why he was so protective of Janet. Not that she was frail or helpless. She, too, worked on the farm and had raised four strong healthy boys, two of which, Ian and Fred, were in college. They had been born ten months apart and, due to the cutoff times for school entry, they were in the same grade. Ian had resented it until high school when they had become friends, and both were now going to Concordia College in Seward, Nebraska. The oldest, Brian, was working the farm with his father and would likely inherit it. He was engaged to be married next year and was building a house across the creek from the old farmhouse for them to live in. The youngest, Lawrence, was still in high school. Maddy's and Janet's kids had been in school and youth group together, and, although Maddy and Janet were not especially close, they were friends.

Janet leaned over as Maddy sat down and whispered "Did you hear about that man, in the park?

I'm glad we're out on the farm, away from all the crime in town."

Maddy smiled to herself at the mention of the 'crime' in town and remembered that Janet was known to be a bit overprotective of her family. *But then*, she thought, *what mother wasn't?* "Sometimes isolation can mean vulnerability rather than safety," she said.

"Oh, you would think of something like that!" Janet said exasperatedly, but she was smiling, too. She knew Maddy often played devil's advocate just to get the conversational ball rolling. They turned their attention to the meeting.

Maddy focused her attention, trying to keep straight the difference between the graphs of past year's flood levels and those showing projected flood levels under different conditions. Fortunately, the church and parsonage were on higher ground, but if members of the congregation got flooded out, they would help by offering their guest room and helping with clean up efforts.

Mayor Weatherby had gotten up now and was outlining what the city planned to do, but it was pretty much the same as last year. He summed up and asked for questions, but after years of flood preparations, everyone pretty much knew what to do.

Someone two rows ahead of them raised his hand and was recognized.

"What about that murdered guy in the park? What's being done about that? Have they identified him yet?" It was Lucien Kenner, the owner and editor of the local weekly paper, the *Advocate*. Due to the fact that he had a staff of one, he was also reporter, investigator, and photographer. His spinster sister, Gabrielle, held down the little office, answered the phone, and typed up everything from feature stories to obituaries and want ads on their single computer. Lucien and Gabby shared a strong family resemblance that Maddy supposed came from their French-Canadian background—delicate features, long sharp noses, and curly hair the color that is often called 'dishwater blond'. Lucien had a perpetually surprised expression that came from his nearly invisible blond eyelashes and mildly exophthalmic eyes that fit perfectly with his constant attitude of curiosity. Maddy wasn't sure if the curiosity propelled him into journalism or if being a reporter enhanced his curiosity.

There was a lot of shifting and murmuring as people whose attention had wandered were pulled back by this new and salacious topic.

"I'm going to let Sheriff Buchholz talk about that, as he is conducting the investigation." said the mayor and sat down.

Joe stood up and began "Those of you who have read this morning's *Advocate* know that the body of a strangled man was found last Saturday in Riverfront Park. As the park is outside the city limits, I'll be conducting the investigation in full cooperation with the Marshallhaven police." He nodded at Chief Hanson, who nodded back. Maddy figured that the sheriff's department would investigate no matter where the murder had occurred because the Marshallhaven Police Department consisted of two traffic officers who patrolled the town for speeders and rowdy partiers.

Joe continued, "Just this afternoon we got a positive identification from his fingerprints. His name was Zachariah Hendergast, and apparently, he used to live here about 30 years ago." As he said the man's name, a buzz erupted as people began whispering and shifting in their seats. "If anyone remembers him or can shed any light on why he has returned…" he began, but stopped as an older man in the front row with an impressive comb over and bib overalls raised his hand and interrupted.

"I remember him, Sheriff! He was that hippie that made that ugly twisted metal sculpture stuff and traveled around trying to sell it."

His wife yanked him down into his seat again saying "Hush, Abe, you can tell him about it after the meeting."

But Joe was saying "No, please, if you can tell me any more about him, it could really help the investigation. Did he have any family?"

Sarah, the owner of the bakery, got up with a disapproving sniff and began to speak. "He was a traveling artist and worked in the drug store. He disappeared around '82 and good riddance, I said. I have no idea why he'd come back."

Abe had stood up again despite his wife's protestations. "He was a no account by most reckoning, but nothing that you could really point to. He didn't drink or at least he wasn't a drunk. He smoked like a chimney, though, and lived in that shabby camper truck, making his so-called 'art', traveling around to shows in the summer and coming back in the winter to make more of it. I don't know as he had any family. He worked in the drug store stocking shelves and stuff during the winter, like Sarah said. I guess being an artist don't pay much. Or I should say the sculpture didn't. He did nice stained-glass, though, and if you all remember, he did all the stained-glass for St. Paul's when they rebuilt the church after that fire. Anyways, he must have figured he could settle down with the money he earned from that, 'cause he just disappeared the next year, and nobody seen him since." He sat down with a satisfied expression. A lot of heads were nodding, but no one seemed to have any more to add.

"No one saw him, until last weekend, that is," Joe was saying. "Did anyone else see him last week?" His question was greeted with blank looks and shaking heads. "Well, thank you folks. We know this is a disturbing event and we're doing all we can to find the killer and bring him or her to justice. If anyone thinks of anything else that might shed some light on the victim's actions or whereabouts prior to last weekend, please let me know."

Talk was animated as everyone left the meeting. So that's who did the stained-glass, Maddy mused. It certainly was beautiful. Funny how the same artist could produce both lovely church windows and shapeless modern sculptures. She'd have to take a closer look at the windows. Maybe she could learn something about the creator by studying the creation. It was also interesting that the 'unknown' stranger was apparently known to quite a few people in town.

And it occurred to her that the murder did have a connection to the church after all.

CHAPTER FIVE

"So, shall we eat lunch first, or do you want to practice your sermon first?" Maddy asked. Saturdays were workdays for pastors, unlike the rest of the world. Jack looked at his watch.

"Let's see, it's 11 o'clock. I have a quick phone call to return, then let's eat lunch, and I'll go over my sermon after that."

"OK" said Maddy. "I'll help Laura while you're making your call." Laura was the church secretary. She was pleasingly plump with graying blond hair and perpetually sad expression due to her mouth and eyes turning down at the corners. She was actually a very cheerful person who took life as it came. Until Maddy had learned to not be alarmed at her expression, she had frequently asked her what was wrong. Finally, she realized that her face just looked melancholy. Laura looked up dolefully from folding bulletins when Maddy entered her office.

"Would you like some help?" Maddy asked.

"I never turn down any help that's cheerfully offered," she answered with a sad little smile.

"So, have you heard any more about Mr. Hendergast?" Maddy asked as they assembled folded bulletins with their inserts. Laura was one of those people that seemed to know everything that was going on, although Maddy had no idea where she got her information. She spent about thirty hours a week in the church office and seemed to spend the rest at home taking care of her husband, Ronald, who had early Alzheimer's.

"Well, his reappearance in town has certainly stirred up people's emotions, and not just because he was murdered," said Laura with a crinkle in her forehead. "Zachariah Hendergast wasn't exactly universally beloved, you know."

"Actually, I don't know. That was long before we moved here." Maddy thought ruefully that she had been about twenty years old at the time, and suddenly felt young.

"Hmmm. Yes, well, he was what some people called a 'free spirit' and others called a shiftless, aging hippie."

"I kind of gathered from Sarah's and Abe's descriptions that they would agree he fell into the latter category," remarked Maddy.

"You'd think that only if you weren't around back then." Laura's mouth turned down at one corner and her eyes twinkled. "At least when it comes to Sarah's opinion of him. But back then, she was all for that 'free love' sort of thing. Yes, she and Zachariah were quite an item. Didn't try to hide the fact, either, and shocked a lot of people in town. We're still a conservative bunch despite feminism and the sexual revolution and all that."

Maddy chuckled quietly. They certainly were. Not that she didn't hold the same conservative values. But the townspeople had all the family values and morals that made people want to move here from the cities and all the self-righteousness to go along with the values that made the people want to leave. The news that Sarah and Zachariah had been involved was certainly a surprise, though. Not at all what she'd expected after Thursday's meeting. A woman scorned?

"Thanks for your help" said Laura as she stacked the last of the bulletins.

"No, problem. I'll see if Jack is ready for lunch now. See you tomorrow!"

Maddy tried to walk quietly on the tiled floor of the hall as she headed around the corner to the 'Pastor's Study' but could hear that he was still on the phone. Sound carried in the empty corridor and she heard Jack saying, "Harold, if you won't tell me who supposedly didn't like my sermon last week, how am I supposed to talk to them and iron out any misunderstandings?" He paused. "I intimidate them? Hmmm. So what do you want me to do?" He paused again and chuckled. "Uh hungh. I think you're the one who didn't like my sermon, Harold. I'd be happy to talk to you about it whenever you'd like to come in."

Maddy realized that she was eavesdropping and moved quietly past the study door toward the narthex. 'Harold' had to be Harold Broomfield and it sounded like he was up to his old tricks again. Maddy was nursing some unfavorable thoughts and feelings about Harold but put them out of her mind with a little effort. Jack didn't seem to be too perturbed about him. It wasn't her job to deal with him, thank goodness.

As she wandered into the church, she took in the stained-glass twinkling in the late morning sunlight. The church had that serene quiet that all empty churches seem to have. Everything was still except for the flicker of the flame in the eternal light.

There were side aisles between the pews and the windows on each side and she walked slowly up and down looking at each frame, taking in the overall impressions. *They were really good work*, she thought. The size of the panes was small enough to make interesting patterns, but not so small as to look busy or detract from the color or the picture. The colors were vibrant and the depictions were expressive. She noticed that the animals and people were very lifelike, especially the hands and feet, which so often look stiff or unnatural. Hendergast certainly had talent. He seemed to bring out the life in the scenes. The people, animals, even the plants, were alive. Perhaps the moniker of a 'free spirit' was apt for someone who seemed to love life so much. She was admiring the many animals in the Noah's Ark window when she saw it again. It was the outline of a spray bottle. She could see the spray coming from the nozzle. She stepped forward and frowned as she examined it more closely. Even up close she could see that it didn't just 'resemble' a spray bottle or 'evoke the image' of a spray bottle. All the features were there if you looked closely enough.

A thought occurred to her. *What if there were other hidden pictures in the other windows?* She started looking at the other windows more closely but didn't really see anything until the last one. It depicted the Fall of the Wall of Jericho. All of the bricks were basically rectangular except one. Down in the corner, one brick was oddly shaped. The top and bottom were flat, but the sides curved in and the bottom was narrower than the top. And it wasn't symmetrical. The right upper corner extended out further than the left. She stood back and squinted her eyes a little. It looked like an anvil.

"Is it time for an eye exam?" Jack whispered a few inches from her ear.

Maddy jumped and gasped. "Don't sneak up on me like that!"

"Sorry. I didn't mean to scare you," he said with a little smile, "but you do seem to be having trouble focusing."

"No, I'm deliberately squinting. Trying to blur out distractions. Here, take a look" she said pointing to the Wall of Jericho, "What does that look like to you?"

Jack looked at it for a good moment. "Well, I guess it kind of looks like an anvil, but I suppose it's just what my mind is creating out of an oddly shaped stone."

"That's what I would have thought, too," said Maddy, "but look at this!" She showed him the spray bottle. "What does that look like?"

"Huh," muttered Jack with a little frown. He really wanted to say it looked like half an elephant, but he just couldn't.

"Well?" pressed Maddy.

"OK, it looks like a spray bottle," he finally said. "So, what are saying? That these things really are what they look like? That it means something? What could it possibly mean?"

"I don't know" said Maddy slowly, "I don't know."

"Let's go have lunch. I'm famished" said Jack, taking her hand.

"OK" she smiled and squeezed his hand. She could ponder the deep mysteries of spray bottles and anvils later.

Three hours later, Maddy was restless. She'd cleaned up after lunch, listened to Jack's sermon twice, and the chicken and rice casserole for dinner was ready to pop in the oven. Jack was finishing up his preparations for Bible study and would be home in about an hour. She sat down at her computer hoping to find an interesting blog post, or better yet, an e-mail. Sure enough, a letter from Joanna had shown up in her inbox.

To: channelingkatie@cable.com

From: adaspira@mit.edu

Subject: ID

Hi, Mom!

You know I told you that my thesis prof wants me as his teaching assistant for Astronomy 301 next Fall? Well, I was talking to him yesterday about the syllabus and which lectures he'll let me give, and he agreed to let me teach intelligent design as long as I didn't mention God and also present the arguments for evolution. I'm so excited! The students will be able to evaluate the evidence and make up their own minds. I'll have the summer to outline the lectures and get his approval on their content. Let me know if you or Dad know of any resources in the Synod. My prof knows he's probably going to get some flak for letting me teach ID, but he's tenured, so he doesn't have to worry about being fired, and he said he'll back me up to the hilt. In a way, I'm also looking forward to any controversy as a chance to engage people in apologetics. Maybe give them something to think about.

Talk to you later.

Love,

Joanna

Over dinner, Maddy told Jack about Joanna's e-mail.

"Sure," he said "I can put her in touch with someone at the Synod's education committee. Although, I'm pretty sure that their work falls under the heading of Creation Science, which isn't quite the same thing as Intelligent Design. Still I'm sure they have some resources that she can use. That's exciting!"

"Uh, uh, uh" he said as Andante tried her usual dinnertime trick of hopping into a chair and sniffing at the food as closely as she could without actually being on the table. She innocently looked over at the bookcase as if the food in front of her were the last thing on her mind.

"Andante, Down!" said Maddy firmly, and she jumped down, landing with a heavy thump. As a seventeen-pound Maine Coon, she wasn't terribly dainty, but she did have the most adorable expression as she begged shamelessly from the floor.

"How come she obeys you and not me?" asked Jack.

"It's all in the tone" said Maddy. "Cats are a lot like kids. They have to know you mean it the first time."

CHAPTER SIX

With a flourish, Maddy dispensed the last of the egg yolk filling into the deviled eggs for the potluck after worship. She popped them in the fridge, touched up her lips with her favorite 'Spicy Peach' lipstick, noted the time, and headed over to the church in time for Sunday morning Bible study.

As she was closing the door, she hesitated. Should she lock it? She'd never locked it before, yet a murderer was still on the loose. In fact, the police had no real leads yet at all. But a murderer wouldn't be interested in an empty house would he? Unless he would use it as an opportunity to hide out and wait until the owners got home. Besides, hadn't she reasoned that the murderer was probably specifically connected to Hendergast and that the murder was not likely to have been random? But Hendergast has a connection to the church, and so, definitely, did she and Jack. On the other hand, would changing her behavior out of fear be giving in to that fear? Were other people doing the same? Had the community changed? Realizing that she might be standing outside her front door all morning if she didn't make a decision, she impulsively turned the lock and pulled the door closed. Only when she was halfway across the parking lot did she realize she'd left her purse, with her keys, on the kitchen counter. Sigh. Jack would have his keys on him.

It was another sunny Sunday morning. She had managed to keep quiet in Bible study, but maybe that was only because the topic had kept away from the more controversial subjects. She basked in the warmth, but she kept her eyes away from the windows during worship. She was not, definitely *not*, going to repeat last Sunday's embarrassment. It was when she was filing out after service that she sneaked a quick peek at Noah's Ark and the Wall of Jericho. The spray bottle and the anvil were still there. She must take some time later to come over and study the others. What if there were more anomalies?

She waited until Jack had greeted all the parishioners before asking for his house keys. He handed them over with a raised eyebrow.

"You locked the door? I didn't think you ever locked the front door unless we were going out of town or something."

"I know" she answered, looking sheepish, "but with this murder and all, I guess I'm feeling, well, not exactly nervous, just—you know—like something's not right."

"Well," said Jack seriously, "If locking the front door makes you feel better, go ahead and do it. I'll just have to remember to carry my keys with me at all times." He grinned. "You're not going to lock me out while I'm mowing the grass or anything, are you?" This got a smile from Maddy, as he knew it would. She had actually locked him out once while he was mowing. That was when they'd first moved in, before they realized no one in town bothered to lock their doors.

"I guess I'm being silly" she said.

"No, no, if it makes you feel better, you go ahead and lock the doors," Jack said, serious again. "This is about your peace of mind. There's no 'Thus saith the Lord' about locking or not locking the doors." He gave her a kiss and turned toward the vestry to remove his vestments.

"Sorry I'm a bit late" puffed Maddy as she placed her deviled eggs on the potluck table. She was about to explain about locking herself out of her house, but realized that no one was listening. The church kitchen was gleaming and modern, and large enough to hold quite a large group of gossipers. The buzz in the kitchen was entirely about the murder. It had made front page news, above the fold, in the *Advocate*, as she knew it would. After all, it was the biggest news since last year when Velma Vorderstrasse won the blue ribbon at the Iowa State Fair for her hand-crocheted antimacassars. "MURDER IN THE PARK," the headline screamed. Yet the article provided no new information despite its length. Except the picture. They had dug up a picture of Zachariah Hendergast from thirty years ago and printed it next to a picture of the park, sans corpse. He had long, frizzy dirty-blond hair in a pony tail, a long untrimmed beard, and an engaging smile full of tobacco-stained teeth. He looked exactly as Maddy had expected from the descriptions she'd been given, both of his appearance and his personality. The gossip about him was flying today, that was for sure. Maddy guiltily thought maybe she should be the good pastor's wife and tell people they shouldn't gossip, but the possibility of learning something worthwhile was too tempting.

She edged quietly into the kitchen, but that was a mistake.

"Oh, Maddy, I made you some decaf coffee!" said Marlene upon spotting her. Maddy hated church coffee. It tasted like weak, tepid, smelly sock water. She couldn't quite decide if it was the huge can of grocery store ground coffee absurdly rationed to one cup of grounds per fifty-cup percolator, the unfiltered tap water, or the aged percolators themselves, stained with the rancid oils of years of coffee, that slowly but surely burnt the coffee throughout the worship service. She was a coffee snob, no doubt about it. At home, they ground their own beans, and then brewed it with filtered water in a drip coffee maker into an insulated carafe so that it wouldn't spend so much as a minute on a warming plate. She had avoided church coffee for a long time by saying that she only drank decaf, which was true. As most of the over-fifty crowd insisted that coffee without caffeine just wasn't coffee, she'd been safe.

Then Marlene, sweet and considerate woman that she was, had dug up a smaller twenty-cup percolator from who knows where, labeled it "DECAF" in prominent letters, bought some decaf coffee of the same grocery store brand as the regular, and begun making decaf especially for her.

Maddy smiled and accepted the Styrofoam cup. It was wretched stuff, but she couldn't let Marlene suspect. "Thank you! That's so sweet of you" she said with convincing sincerity. She noticed Babs carefully attending to the communion ware at the back sink. Babs, Barbara Rorschach, arranged all the church flowers, donating the lovely blooms from her sizeable greenhouse. She also organized the altar guild, educated the volunteers, and filled in whenever there was a gap in guild coverage.

"I've noticed that some of the younger adults are opting for the decaf as well," Marlene put in helpfully. Maddy had noticed that, too. She'd also noticed that they didn't come back for seconds.

"Now, that Zachariah Hendergast, he was always saying that coffee was bad for you, and everyone should be drinking herbal tea," Marlene was saying. "But now I heard on the news that coffee has antioxidants and is good for you, after all!" Maddy listened half-attentively, taking the smallest sips she possibly could of her coffee. She had accepted it black, knowing that adding the presweetened, nondairy creamer from the large containers next to the percolators just made it worse.

"Did you talk to him often? Zachariah Hendergast, I mean. Did he attend church?" she asked.

"He did come a few times when he started working on the windows. That was when we were worshiping at St. Andrew's, the Episcopalian church. I mean in their building, you know, when our church was being rebuilt, not, you know, worshiping with them..." Marlene hastily added, lest anyone should think that they'd attended an Episcopalian church service.

"I know what you mean" said Maddy quickly, trying not to smile. "That was very kind of them to let St. Paul's use their building."

"Oh, yes. Yes, it was," said Marlene, "but Zachariah didn't come for very long. He kept trying to push his progressive views on everyone and was always starting arguments, and of course, everyone knew he was living in sin with Sarah Anderson. Of course, that was a long time ago, and Sarah has turned over a new leaf. We have to put the best construction on things, don't we," rambled Marlene.

"Yes, we really should," said Maddy trying not to get off track. "What kind of things did he argue about?"

"Well," said Marlene, taking the bit and running with it, "It was usually about politics and social issues, always going on about how we Lutherans weren't loving and tolerant enough, trying to argue the merits of cohabitating and ERA and stuff like that. You know, 'try before you buy' and 'equal pay for equal work' and all that nonsense. But the last time he was here, he got into a real big fight with Lenny Carlisle. It was hard to know what exactly it was about, but Lenny just kept repeating 'You better keep your mouth shut about it'. Someone said later that Zachariah had found out that he was taking a medication that was, you know, embarrassing, him working at the Pharmacy and all, and he was telling people about it. Not very nice, you know, but it hardly helped Lenny to get into a public shouting match about it. But I heard other similar stories. He'd find out something, like who was getting birth control pills, or hemorrhoid medications, or that high powered antibiotic that is used to treat STDs, and then he'd threaten to tell people if they didn't do favors for him. Not that I found out exactly what the medication was that Lenny was taking. I don't like to pry into other people's private affairs."

"No, of course not" murmured Maddy, still desperately trying not to smile. She was surprised, though. Lenny, shouting? It wasn't like him. It must have been something really embarrassing.

"Did anyone like him?" asked Maddy.

"Well, he and Harold Broomfield seemed to get along pretty well. They liked to talk on about how 'the church must change or die', whatever that means. I mean, the church has been pretty much unchanged for centuries and it's still around."

Maddy nodded. By this time she had choked down about half of the coffee and didn't think she could take any more. She saw Elmer Martin heading toward the coffee table, and she just didn't feel like talking to him. Part of it was embarrassment from having corrected him in Bible study last week, but the other part was that she just didn't like him. She gritted her teeth every time he started in with one of his smug little analogies, and she just wasn't in the mood for another one.

"You know, I think I should help clear up some of the tables," she said and quickly moved away, leaving the half-full Styrofoam cup behind.

It certainly seemed as if Zachariah Hendergast had made plenty of enemies. For starters, there was Sarah. He had just up and left her. 'Good riddance' was what she'd said. Was she still angry at him? Enough to kill him? Then there was Lenny and anyone else who had been blackmailed. Could he have found out something that was not just embarrassing, but enough to kill for? How about Sarah's father? She would have been in her very early twenties at the time. Might he have thought that Hendergast had corrupted his daughter? How about other parents? Frankly, there didn't seem to be anyone who remembered him fondly. And yet, those things happened thirty years ago—water under the bridge, so to speak.

Maddy went into the kitchen to help wash dishes. Babs had finished rinsing the individual cups into a plastic tub which she would pour onto the bushes outdoors and was now arranging the clean communion ware onto a platter to return to the sacristy. Maddy filled the sink with water and began washing the tableware and mugs.

The conversation had shifted to gardening and when was the best time to start tomatoes. It was the same conversation every year—predicting the last killing frost, whether or not to start plants indoors and transplant them, how much rainfall there had been so far that Spring and how much watering would need to be done. She listened with interest. Babs was talking about her flowers. Maddy usually grew tomatoes, squash, onions, carrots, bell peppers, and watermelons. Maybe not watermelons this year. With the kids gone, it was hard for her and Jack to eat a whole melon. Maybe cantaloupe. They were smaller.

She pulled the plug in the sink to drain the dishwater, dried her hands, picked up her egg container, and said her goodbyes. On the way home, her mind wandered back to the murder. Pursuing suspects in this town would be like looking for a needle in a haystack. She didn't envy the police that job. But on the other hand, she did think there might be something to the windows. Zachariah had made the windows and if there were more obvious anomalies, he must have intended something by them. *Like the theory behind Intelligent Design,* she thought, remembering Joanna's e-mail. When you encounter evidence of design that could not have happened by chance, then it must have a design, and by inference, a designer. And you could know something of the designer by looking at the designed. She would definitely have to look closer at those stained-glass windows. Tomorrow. Tonight was movie night, her weekly 'date' with Jack. No, not tomorrow. Monday was Jack's day off. Tuesday, then, in the morning before going to lunch with Penny.

She looked up to see Jack headed towards her from his office. She waited for him; then, hand in hand, they walked home.

They had almost finished their light supper of BLTs and chunky tomato soup, when the phone rang.

"Hello?"

"Oh, Mom! I've got to talk to you. Do you have time?" It was Martha and she was sounding upset.

Maddy was quick to answer, "Of course, I have the time! What's wrong? Is it the baby?"

"No, no, the baby's fine. It's just… well… did you crave strange things when you were pregnant?"

"Sure, I ate all kinds of weird things. Usually strong flavors, like raw onions, or strange combinations like cinnamon rolls and pickles. Why? Have you been craving odd things?"

"Mmmm-hmmm. But I've never heard of anything like this."

"Well, what have you been eating?"

Martha hesitated. "Well it all started this morning. You know how hectic things can be on Sunday morning." Maddy knew full well that Sunday mornings in a pastor's home were not like Sunday mornings anywhere else. She murmured assent and Martha continued.

"Well, Harlan's been trying to help me out as much as possible as well as get everything ready for service, and he was making breakfast and he burned the toast.

Not just a little dark, but burnt black with smoke pouring out of the toaster. I think the toaster's dead. It was probably on its last legs anyway." Maddy made a mental note that a new toaster would make a nice gift for them. They were like many young couples, making do with secondhand furniture and appliances until they could afford better.

Martha was continuing her saga, "So Harlan was getting flustered and dumped the burnt toast in the sink so he could keep his attention on the eggs, and, and, ... now this is the bizarre part... it smelled so good. I was just getting up and said 'What smells so good?' and he said 'I'm doing the best I can. There's no need to get sarcastic!' I guess he thought I was being a smart aleck or something. But I wasn't! I went into the kitchen and took the burnt toast out of the sink and ate it. Then he thought I was trying to be nice and not hurt his feelings that he burnt the toast, but it really tasted good! So, I got out the bread and burnt some more toast and ate it. That's when the toaster kind of pinged and sparked and went dead. And now I want some more burnt toast and I can't have any because I blew up the toaster making burnt toast this morning!" she finished with a wail.

Maddy was having a hard time not laughing. "I think the toaster was probably malfunctioning when

Harlan burnt the first batch of toast. It wasn't your fault," she said reassuringly.

"But Mom! What about my eating burnt toast? Is that bad? Is something wrong?" This time Maddy did laugh.

"It's not funny!" said Martha, nearly in a panic by now.

"No, I'm not laughing at you. You're just fine. I was laughing at some of the things I ate during my pregnancies. I ate worse things than burnt toast."

"Like what?" Martha was calming down.

"Well, I suppose the worst was one night when I was pregnant with Joanna. I woke up in the middle of the night just starving. I didn't want to wake you or Jack, so I got up quietly in the dark and didn't turn on any lights. I just went into the kitchen and cut myself a piece of strawberry rhubarb pie that we had leftover from a few nights ago and sat down and savored it with just the moonlight coming in the window. I thought it was the best tasting piece of pie I had ever tasted, so I had another piece. When I finished, I just put the dishes in the sink and went back to bed."

"What's so strange about strawberry rhubarb pie? That sounds pretty normal to me," Martha said, confused.

"You'll know in a minute," said Maddy, and continued. "The next morning, I remembered that piece of pie and thought another piece sounded really good. So I went into the kitchen, and uncovered the pie, and it was covered in mold. Not just a couple spots, but thickly covered—green and fuzzy. I knew it had to have been there the night before as well. Of course, I couldn't bring myself to eat it knowing the mold was there, but, oh, it had tasted good the night before."

Martha was revolted. "Ugh. I can't believe you didn't notice! Oh, that's disgusting! I'm not going to start eating moldy stuff, am I?" she asked, suddenly worried again.

"Well, let's just say I recommend not eating in the dark," said Maddy, laughing.

"I can't talk about food anymore," said Martha, "but I do have a question about sleeping. I can't sleep on my back anymore because the pressure makes my legs go numb, but when I sleep on my side, the baby pulls my stomach down so much my back starts to hurt. I also feel like I take up the whole bed, although

Harlan is too nice to mention it. He just looks so stiff crowded next to the edge like that."

"Oh, I always used a little flat pillow under the side of my stomach to relieve the strain, but I don't know what to tell you about bed space." Their full sized bed, as opposed to a queen-sized which would have given Harlan a little more room, was another of their hand-me-down furniture that they were making do with.

Martha sighed. "Oh, well, it will only be for another month."

Maddy laughed again. "Then you still won't be sleeping well, but it will be due to midnight feedings instead of uncomfortable positions!"

"Thanks," said Martha drily, "You sure know how to cheer a person up." But Maddy could tell she was smiling. It was a good sign that she no longer sounded panicked. "Well, I'd better let you go. Thanks for listening and for the suggestions."

"Anytime. Love you!" Maddy hung up with a smile, thinking of her new grandbaby on the way. She pulled out the hot air popcorn popper and set it up in preparation for their movie.

She'd pulled an old favorite from their collection of DVDs—*The Shop Around the Corner,* the old black and white Jimmy Stewart movie that *You've Got Mail* was loosely based on. She and Jack munched happily on popcorn and laughed as the two main characters exchanged anonymous love letters, while squabbling in the shop they worked at together—never realizing the person they couldn't stand in real life was the fantasy lover they were writing to. They laughed harder as each plot twist contrasted their real and dream lives.

Maddy mused abstractedly in the back of her mind about the murder. What if one of the sweet, kind people she knew were someone else on the inside—someone capable of murder? She shook her head. No, *The Shop Around the Corner* was a comedy that depended on fantastic and absurd plot twists. People couldn't really live such a double life.

CHAPTER SEVEN

The sun shone in the bedroom window. It was almost 9:30 a.m. and Maddy and Jack were awake but still lounging in bed, just talking and being close. Sleeping in on Monday was such a treat.

"So, what shall we do today? Go for a walk? Till the garden? Go to Des Moines and take in a matinee?"

"Mmmm" said Jack, "Can we do all three?"

Maddy laughed, "Glutton for punishment, are you? We don't have time for all three, but we haven't been to Des Moines lately. Maybe there's something good at the IMAX."

Just then the doorbell rang. Maddy looked despairingly at Jack. "Not again." She threw on a robe and slippers and went to answer the door while Jack pulled on jeans and sweatshirt. She peeked around the door, knowing her hair must be frightful.

"I'm really sorry to bother you. I know it's Pastor's day off and all, but I thought he'd want to know." It was Roy Zabel, one of the trustees.

"Know what?" asked Maddy, relaxing. Roy wouldn't care if her hair looked like a tornado had hit it. He was always so kind.

"Some kids must have been playing baseball across the street and hit a ball through one of the church windows," he said, holding out the offending ball. "Went clear through the empty tomb."

"Oh, no," said Maddy, "Not one of the stained-glass windows!"

"I'll come over and look at it," said Jack who had materialized behind her looking as if he'd been up and dressed for hours. *How did he do that?* Maddy thought. She looked again at the baseball.

"Could I look at that a minute?" she asked.

"Sure" he said and handed it to her. It looked new. Not just new, but pristine. If kids had been playing with it, it hadn't been long. It had never been hit with a bat or dropped in the dirt. Come to think of it, there weren't any scratches on it either, or pieces of embedded glass.

She looked up at Jack. "You might want to call the police," she said, and then explained her line of thinking. "This ball hasn't been played with, and hasn't broken any windows, either."

Jack took the ball and stared at it, his forehead wrinkling. "You're right. Roy, why don't you show me exactly where you found this?"

They headed over to the church and Maddy went to shower and change. Something was bothering her. If someone deliberately broke the window, they might use a new ball, but then why no glass or scratches? Why would someone break a window, and then toss the ball through? Why not just throw the ball through the window?

"...over there behind that pew", Roy was saying as Maddy walked into the nave. Joe was there already and was looking at the ball in his hand. Lucien Kenner was standing behind him, taking shorthand notes in a flip top notepad. Great. She could see the headline now—MYSTERIOUS MISCREANT VANDA-LIZES CHURCH WINDOWS or something equally sensational.

Lucien had always made her a little uncomfortable, with his peering eyes and nearly invisible blond eyebrows. He wasn't exactly rude, just a bit pushy when pursuing a story. *Still,* Maddy thought, *he was just doing his job.* She supposed that vandalism to a church was big news in a sleepy town like Marshallhaven. She smiled and turned her attention to the others.

"There she is," Roy was saying, "Mrs. Mitchell, why don't you tell the sheriff what you said about the ball being all clean and such." Maddy smiled to herself. Few people besides children called her Mrs. Mitchell anymore. But Roy was old school, unfailingly polite, and somehow it didn't seem stiff or standoffish when he said "Mr." and "Mrs."

She turned to Joe and started explaining about how the ball had no rubs, marks, or scratches and therefore had never been marred by a bat or by a window.

"I can see that," said Joe. "What do you think happened?"

"Well," answered Maddy, trying to ignore Lucien's furious scribbling, "It looks to me like the window was broken first and the ball thrown through the hole to make it look like an accident."

Blood Stained

"If the perpetrator wanted it to really look like an accident, why not just throw it through the window?" Joe asked.

"I…, I don't know" said Maddy, slowly. Actually, she had a kind of idea, but she needed to think it through. And she didn't want to voice all of her ideas in front of Lucien, who was peering at her with undisguised curiosity.

"For what it's worth, I agree with you," said Joe, seriously. "That hole", he said pointing to the broken window, a depiction of the Resurrection and the Empty Tomb, "was not made by a single impact. It's irregular and was probably made by two or three hits."

A light bulb went on in Maddy's mind as she pictured someone hitting the window. If someone was hitting the window with their fist or an object, they were aiming for a particular spot. It had to do with the anomalies. She knew it. But she had only found two and in other windows, and she thought it would sound outlandish if she said it out loud. Jack was looking at her pointedly, but she didn't say anything.

"Well, I'll look into this, and have the patrol officers swing by a few more times. If there's any more suspicious activity, let me know." Joe headed to the back of the church. Roy turned to follow and was intercepted by Lucien.

"So you found the baseball and the broken window?" he asked. "Could you show me where?" Roy politely turned back towards the pews and pointed to the spot on the floor. Lucien snapped pictures of the pews and the broken window. Then he turned to Jack and Maddy.

"Do you have any idea who could have done this? Why would someone want to break this window?" He gazed unblinkingly at Maddy.

"We don't have any idea," said Jack smoothly.

"What did you mean by what you were saying earlier?" Lucien asked, still staring at Maddy. She was sure he had to blink sometime, but, as of yet, she still hadn't seen it. *Wouldn't his eyes get dried out?* she wondered. "Um, I'm not sure what you mean," she answered slowly.

"About someone breaking the window first and then throwing the ball through. Can I quote you on that?"

Maddy cringed. She didn't want to be quoted in the newspaper, but she didn't see how she could avoid it. At least Lucien was meticulous about quoting people accurately. He had done several small articles in the past on things like the church's celebration of Easter and quotes from Jack on holidays like Memorial Day and the Fourth of July. He could also spell, punctuate, and construct grammatically correct sentences, which was more than she could say about a lot of other journalists at larger papers like the Des Moines Register, the Minneapolis Tribune, and even the New York Times. There were worse things than being quoted in the Marshallhaven Advocate.

"It was just an idea," she said a little lamely. "I haven't really thought it out, yet."

Lucien nodded and smiled. He flipped back a page of his notebook and read, *"It looks to me like the window was broken first and the ball thrown through the hole to make it look like an accident." Sheriff Buchholz agreed, noting that the window was broken in such a way to suggest multiple impacts.* He looked at Maddy for approval.

She was impressed. "Uh, yeah, that's OK." She gave him what she hoped was a polite smile.

"Thanks. I'll just be going then." And he shuffled out of the church, still hunched over his notepad.

"You coming?" asked Jack to Maddy, who was trailing behind.

"Um, I'll be along soon." She wanted to look at the rest of the windows.

Joe turned back as Jack approached and asked, "Have you given any more thought as to who might have known Zachariah Hendergast in the past or knew why he was back in town?"

"No, sorry," said Jack. "I've been busy, and it slipped my mind. Stan will probably know. I understand that he was involved with the rebuilding of the church. Come to think of it, Stan probably knew Hendergast himself. I wonder why he didn't recognize him from the photograph?"

"It's not that surprising, actually," said Joe. "After all, it's been thirty years. And, um, let's just say that death by strangulation distorts the facial features." Jack and Maddy both winced but nodded.

"Yes, well, I'll ask Stan who else interacted with Zachariah. Maybe someone will remember something important," said Jack. "I hope so," said Joe, "A lot of people in town remember him, and either admired or detested him, but no one wants to admit being an actual friend or even a moderate acquaintance." The men left the nave and Maddy heard the goodbyes as they went their separate ways. She turned back to the windows and started looking for anomalies.

After about fifteen minutes she found what was probably another one. In the Nativity window, hidden in the straw of the stable, was the outline of two crossed candy canes. There were even lines for the red and white peppermint striping, although they were straw colored in the window. She pulled a little notebook out of her purse and wrote: Noah's Ark: Spray Bottle, Fall of Jericho: Anvil, Nativity: Candy Canes.

She went back to searching the windows with renewed enthusiasm, but, an hour and a half later, she had found nothing else. She looked at her watch and gasped. It was after twelve. She closed up the church and rushed back to the parsonage.

"I'm sorry, Jack! I lost track of time," she said hurriedly, "I'll get lunch together. Is there anything you would particularly like?" she asked. To her relief Jack was grinning.

"Still searching the windows for secret messages?" he asked. She nodded.

"Find any?" he asked again.

"Um, well, yes, actually, I found a pair of candy canes in the Nativity window," said Maddy.

Jack looked thoughtful. "I have to admit that they don't appear to be random coincidence. But as for meaning...?" He shook his head. "You think it's some kind of message put there by Zachariah Hendergast?"

"I don't know what they mean," said Maddy, "but they're there and Hendergast had to have put them there." She hesitated but plunged on. "I think that whoever broke that window was trying to obliterate part of the pattern."

"If that's true," said Jack, "then he or she might not stop at breaking windows."

Maddy looked worried, but then said, "But no one knows that I'm looking at the windows for these anomalous pictures."

"Someone knows something. Someone tried to obliterate a particular part of a window. Or I should say, succeeded," said Jack. "Be careful who you talk to about this."

"What about Penny?" asked Maddy.

"I think we can safely say Penny isn't a murderer or a vandal," said Jack with a more light-hearted laugh. Maddy relaxed and turned to start lunch, but a part of her mind wondered if they could safely say anything about anyone anymore. First a murder, then a deliberately broken window. Her safe, quiet little world was changing.

CHAPTER EIGHT

Oh, well, it was too late to go into Des Moines anyway, thought Maddy ruefully as they both changed into work clothes. Just after lunch they'd gotten a call asking for help with sandbagging along the river. There were still some businesses near the waterfront park that were at risk if the water got above moderate flood stage.

Maddy looked at the park as they passed it on the way downtown. Of course, there was nothing to see now, but she could picture in her mind's eye the dark night, a man clutching desperately at the belt around his neck, the lifeless body left under the trees. She shook her head to clear it. No point dwelling on such gruesome thoughts.

There were already people at work when they arrived, and the base of the sandbag wall had already been started. Maddy moved toward the empty lot where people were filling bags. Jack went to do the heavier work of stacking the filled sandbags to build the wall.

Some people were shoveling sand, and some were holding the bags as they were filled. She looked around until she saw someone who didn't seem to have a partner. It was Abe, who had spoken up at the meeting. He was trying to hold a bag and fill it at the same time. His face looked hot a sweaty and his blonde-grey combover had fallen over his eyes. Maddy smiled, picked up an empty bag and held it open so that Abe could fill it. He gratefully put both hands on the shovel and turned to the huge mound of sandy dirt that had been provided.

"At least it's a nice day for working outside," she remarked. Abe grunted as he shoveled dirt into the bag.

"We sure appreciate your help," he said, after silently filling a couple bags. "Some people think that if it's not their house or business in danger that they don't need to help out."

Maddy was indignant. "The community is everyone's responsibility! What if these shops went out of business due to flood damage? What then? People would lose their jobs, and no one would be providing the service that they do, that's what!"

"I know. You're preaching to the choir," said Abe with a gruff laugh. Maddy looked around. There were actually quite a few people helping out. It looked like most people felt the way she and Abe did after all. She calmed down a bit and put the full sandbag on the pile and picked up another bag.

"So, what do you remember about Zachariah Hendergast?" she asked as Abe started filling the next bag.

Abe grunted again. "Well, mostly what I said at the town meeting. He wasn't well liked, I can tell you that. Worthless piece of ..." He stopped suddenly remembering who he was talking to. He cleared his throat and began again. "He was sly. Thought he was clever. Liked to argue. Thought that if he could get you stumped, then his position must be right. He ruffled a lot of feathers, that's for sure. But that wasn't what really got people upset. He'd find out things and then get people to do special favors for him." Maddy nodded. This wasn't the first time she'd heard about it.

Maddy balanced the filled bag against her shin as she tied it shut with a cord. "Like what?" she asked.

"Well, he'd get people to give him discounts or privileges at their businesses, or 'hire' him to do odd jobs. It didn't seem like out-and-out blackmail, but it felt like it, you know?"

"Are you speaking from personal experience?" she asked carefully. She opened up a fresh bag and braced herself as Abe shoveled the heavy sand into it.

Abe looked at her sideways and his mouth turned down at the corners. "Yeah. He found out that our daughter, Karen, was on them birth control pills. He insinuated that we wouldn't want people to know what she was up to, nudge, nudge, wink, wink. Then 'suggested' that I let him use my farm truck to haul his sculptures around the state to his art shows."

"Did you let him?" Maddy asked.

Abe's face lightened. "No! I just laughed at him. Karen was taking the pills for her acne. She wasn't engaged in any hanky panky. He didn't like that, but what could he do?"

Maddy laughed, too. Hendergast seemed to have been a pest, but if that was all it was, she'd have to look elsewhere for a motive for murder. She placed the latest filled sandbag onto the pallet they were filling just as the forklift trundled over to convey it back to the rising wall.

By 6 p.m., the wall was a decent height and stretched around all the businesses closest to the river. She and Jack would probably be sore tomorrow, but it felt good to have contributed. *That was what community was all about,* she thought. This was why they loved living here. People cared about each other. They pitched in to help out. Sarah had donated doughnuts and coffee for the workers, and Maddy indulged in a large apple fritter as she and Jack sat and watched the river for a bit before heading home. The river was high, already over its banks. If it stayed at this level, things would be OK, but if it rose another five feet, it would hit the sandbag wall. If it rose ten feet, it would be close to the top of the wall and it might not hold back that much water. But the river hadn't gotten that high for twenty years. Only time would tell. She finished off her doughnut just as Jack finished his coffee.

"Some day off, huh?" he said with a smile, and helped her to her feet.

CHAPTER NINE

"So, you found three odd little pictures hidden in the stained-glass windows, you have no idea what they mean, but think they are some kind of message from the guy that made the windows," said Penny skeptically.

It was Tuesday, and Maddy and Penny were having their weekly lunch. "Yep. I can't reach any other logical conclusion. But I can't seem to find any more of the anomalies, as I call them, and I have no idea what they could mean." said Maddy, discouraged.

Penny stabbed a grape tomato from her salad and looked at it thoughtfully. "Remember when you tried to teach me how to do Sudoku puzzles?" she asked.

"Umm, hmm" said Maddy, around a bite of sandwich.

"Well, remember how you said that one big mistake people make in Sudoku is letting your eyes wander randomly around the grid looking for a move to jump out at them…"

"When they should be systematically working from square to square, quadrant to quadrant!" finished Maddy with excitement in her eyes.

Penny paused to chew and swallow her tomato. "It's also kind of like reading x-rays, you need to be systematic in your viewing or you'll miss things," Penny added.

"Of course! I haven't been approaching it systematically at all. Focusing on a small section of the window at a time will also keep away the distraction of the larger picture."

She pulled out her little notebook, flipped to a blank page, and divided it into two five-by-two tables. She then labeled the first block 'Nativity" and underneath it wrote 'Candy Canes'". She then moved to the lower table and in the top third square wrote 'Noah's Ark' and underneath it, 'Spray Bottle'". She moved to the last set of blocks and wrote 'Jericho'" with 'Anvil' underneath it. She then filled in the rest of the windows, and under 'Resurrection' she wrote *broken* in small letters. She smiled in satisfaction at her work.

"I'll go back this afternoon and be more systematic in my search," she said, and put the notebook back into her purse. "So, tell me, how is the health fair coming?"

Penny groaned. "I could really use some help. Could you come early to help set up on Friday?"

"No problem. And you still want me to take blood pressures?" said Maddy.

"Thank you, thank you, thank you!" said Penny fervently.

Maddy actually didn't get a chance to look at the windows until Wednesday evening. That morning, she had baked bread, set a pot roast on the back burner, and paid bills. She thought about taking some time to search for anomalies before lunch, but she didn't have time. She walked across the parking lot to get Jack for lunch. She could have just called him, but she really wanted to get out of the house. It was such a nice day. Was it too good to last? The weather had been wonderful. Warm, sunny, not at all like April in Iowa, which tended to be cold, windy, and rainy. She breathed in the fresh air and the scent of growing things. She'd said something once at a fellowship hour at church about new plant growth smelling different than plants at other times of the year and had been laughed at, but a couple of the old farmers had just nodded sagely as they sipped their coffee.

Things were not that serene inside the church. Angry voices were coming from Jack's office. She paused, torn between wanting to know what was going on, and feeling that she should not eavesdrop. The decision was taken out of her hands when the door flew open and Harold Broomfield stood in the doorway, his back to her. His parting shot was loud enough for anyone in the church, or the whole block for that matter, to hear.

"You're killing this church with your stick in the mud, stubborn, self-righteous ways. What gives you the right to say what we can and can't sing in worship?!" he shouted back into the office.

There was a slight pause and then Jack answered quietly and calmly, "I'm the pastor. It's my job."

"No, it's your job to do what we want. We hired you and we can fire you, you know!" And with that he slammed the office door closed, whipped around and nearly ran Maddy over. He glared at her and opened his mouth as if to say something, then, closed it again into a thin, hard line. Hatred dripped from his eyes as he stormed out the front door.

Maddy was stunned. Why was he mad at *her?* She hadn't done anything to him. Then she was indignant that he'd talked to Jack like that. Who did he think he was? Pastors aren't 'hired'. They are called and can't be 'fired'. And whatever happened to respecting your pastor?

She tapped at the office door, unsure what she would find on the other side. To her surprise, Jack smiled, stood up, and kissed her as if nothing had happened.

"Um, I couldn't help hearing that last. What was that all about?" she asked.

Jack grinned. "Oh, the usual. He wants the church to sing 'Lord of the Dance' on Easter morning in worship. He insisted that it's a traditional Easter hymn."

Maddy wasn't sure whether to laugh or gag. A 'traditional Easter hymn'? She started giggling. "I take it you said 'no'?"

"Hmmm. To put it succinctly, yes. Then he started going on about how I don't listen to anyone and don't take anyone's advice and think I know everything and on and on." Jack was grinning broadly by now.

"Doesn't that worry you? The threat to 'fire' you? I mean, I know he can't do that, but he might turn others against you," Maddy said, suddenly serious.

"I'm not worried," said Jack, more serious now, but still smiling. "He's just one person, and the elders and the council are behind me one hundred percent." He tapped his keyboard to lock it. "So, what's for lunch?"

Maddy finished washing up the lunch dishes and was hanging up the drying towel when the phone rang.

"Hello, Madalyn Mitchell," she answered automatically.

"Mom?"

"Joanna! Hi! What's up?" Maddy took the cordless phone into the living room and settled into the easy chair. She hadn't had a good conversation with Joanna for a while. She liked talking to her second daughter. The two of them were so much alike and had formed a more adult mother-daughter bond after she'd finished high school. Unlike Martha, who still leaned heavily on her mother for support and advice, Joanna talked to Maddy more like a close friend.

But today, her tone was more like Martha's.

"Mom? I, um, want to ask you some questions," she started tentatively. She sounded almost shy.

"Sure, honey. What's on your mind?" said Maddy encouragingly.

"Well, uh, how did you know that Daddy was, you know, 'the one'? How did you know you wanted to marry him and have kids and grow old with him?" she blurted out and then paused expectantly.

"Well, it's a little hard to describe. We had so much in common, and he was easy to talk to. I liked being with him, and as we dated, we talked a lot about what was important to each of us. We shared the same values and the same faith. It wasn't long before I just felt like we belonged together." She had an idea where this was going but didn't push her daughter. She was dying to ask, *So, what's his name?* but she just waited for Joanna to ask more questions or volunteer whatever she was comfortable with.

"So was it like fireworks or you just couldn't stop thinking about him?" Joanna asked.

"I did think about him a lot, when we would see each other next, that kind of thing. I was very much in love, but it was more than that. I didn't just think of him as a great kisser or handsome man, but as a man of integrity that I could both love and respect. I knew that he would take care of me and our children." Maddy was amused at the dreamy tone Joanna's voice had taken on in addition to the hint of shyness. This was not like her at all, usually so logical and business-like. Whoever this guy was, Joanna must be head over heels with him.

"Oh, I just wondered, because, um, I've started seeing someone…" Joanna's voice trailed off in a little lilt.

Maddy had to suppress the urge to say, *No, really??* Instead, she said, "That's wonderful! What's his name?"

"His name's Seamus. Seamus McLaughlin. And it's like you said—I feel like we're meant to be together." Joanna was sounding more and more like a teenager with a crush.

"So, what's he like? Have you met his family?" Maddy felt like she should try to steer her daughter into less emotion-laden waters.

"Oh, he's smart and funny, and soooo good looking. The way he looks at me when we're together, I just melt. I've been waiting for the right man to come along, and I really think it's finally happened. He's an artist—he works with all sorts of media to create the most awe-inspiring pieces. Everything from burlap to old nails, and when he's done with them, it's like, wow! He's just getting started, of course, so he also works nights as a bartender. But once his talent is recognized, he's going to be big!" Joanna finished with a soft sigh.

Nice try, Maddy thought to herself. She decided to try again, a little more pointedly. "Is he a Christian? Do you know what church he goes to?" she asked.

"Oh, of course he's Christian! He said he believes in God and all that. I don't think he goes to church anywhere. He says that he doesn't need church. He talks to God while he's working. Working on his art, I mean. Isn't that neat?" Joanna gushed.

Maddy sighed inwardly. "Does that mean his artwork has a religious theme?" she asked hopefully.

"Well, I'm not really sure what 'theme' any of them have. It's modern art. Each person sees something different in it. That's what makes it so cool."

Maddy tried a different tack. "So, what is he like inwardly? I mean, what are his values, his beliefs, his convictions?"

"Um, well, we haven't really got to that much yet," said Joanna doubtfully.

Maddy wondered what they had gotten to yet, besides his art. She sighed. Joanna was a grown woman now, and she couldn't tell her how to live her life. She and Jack had done their best to instill good values in her while she was growing up, but now the decisions were up to her.

"Honey, I'm so glad you're happy. We'll have to meet him one of these days," said Maddy kindly.

"Oh, Mom, I just know you and Daddy are going to like him. I'm not sure when, but he's dying to meet you, too. I've got a class in about 15 minutes, and I should get going, but, Mom… thanks."

Maddy said goodbye and hung up. So Joanna had a boyfriend. Part of her was glad. Joanna hadn't dated much in high school beyond prom dates. In college, she dated more, but complained that most of the guys were intimidated by someone so focused on academics and career, and frankly by someone who had a higher IQ than they did.

But she also had misgivings about a man who 'didn't need church' and just 'talked to God while he worked' on his art. Oh, well, she'd reserve judgment until she met him. Boy, would she have a lot to talk to Jack with over supper!

On Wednesday evenings, confirmation class was right after school followed by Lenten midweek services. She helped the 7th graders with their memory work while Jack prepped the 8th graders for their public examination coming up on Palm Sunday.

"That's pretty good," she told Jenny, Laura's granddaughter. "Try it again." She was reciting the Fifth Commandment, 'You shall not murder'.

"What does this mean?" Jenny took a deep breath and began, "We should fear and love God, so that we do not hurt or harm our neighbor in his body but help and befriend him in every physical need." Maddy's mind started to wander. *You shall not murder. Someone had. Maybe someone she knew.* She felt sick. *But then, she thought, everyone was capable of murder, just as they were capable of all sins.* Still, it was a very disconcerting thought.

"Very good! OK, now who's next? David, it's your turn. What is the Sixth Commandment?"

"You shall not commit adultery," he said, without hesitation.

"And what does this mean?" she prompted.

"We should fear and love God so that we lead a… a…" He blushed up to the roots of his hair. Maddy waited patiently. "…a *sexually* pure" he whispered and then raised his voice to normal again "and decent life in what we say and do, and husband and wife love and…and…something"

"Honor" prompted Maddy again.

"…honor each other," he finished. He sat down and looked at his hands. *Sarah and Zachariah, living together, or at least sleeping together. That had been a surprise.*

"Good! That was good," said Maddy quickly. "Jonathan, what is the Seventh Commandment?"

Jonathan stood up. "You shall not steal."

"What does this mean?" "We should fear and love God... uh... we do not tell lies...uh...about our neighbor, hurt his...no, uh, slander...uh"

"I think you need to study a little more. You're thinking of the eighth commandment. We'll go on to the next person."

Jonathan nodded and sat down, and she thought she saw a little smirk as he did so. He never seemed to know his memory work. He wasn't dumb. He just spent more energy trying to get out of work than if he'd just done the work to begin with.

"OK, Jenny, do you know the Seventh Commandment?"

Jenny stood up with a superior expression and said loudly, "You shall not steal. We should fear and love God so that we do not take our neighbor's money or possessions, or get them in any dishonest way, but help him to improve and protect his possessions and income." *Someone had deliberately broken the church window.*

"David, your turn again. What is the Eighth Commandment?"

"You shall not give false testimony against your neighbor."

"What does this mean?" said Maddy, feeling like a broken record.

"We should fear and love God so that we do not tell lies about our neighbor, uh, slander… no…betray him, slander him, or hurt his reputation… ummmmm but…" he looked imploringly at Maddy.

"defend…" prompted Maddy.

The light bulb went on and he finished confidently, "…defend him, speak well of him, and explain everything in the kindest way." He sat down with a satisfied plop. *Gossip was running wild. Not just about Hendergast, even allowing that most of it was probably true, but also ugly speculation about who had been blackmailed and about what.*

Something snapped in Maddy. It had been more than a week and gossip and suspicion were running wild. A murderer was still on the loose, and she no longer knew who she could trust, or even who of her friends she really knew anymore. She was going to find out the truth so that life could go back to normal again—leaving her doors unlocked, trusting her neighbors, and not having to worry about vandalism.

Suddenly she realized that the three 7th graders were staring at her expectantly and fidgeting.

"Time to go. Now go meet your parents in the narthex for Lenten Services. Be sure to go over the Ten Commandments again. Next week is Holy Week, so there won't be confirmation class, but the week after we'll move on to the Lord's Prayer."

The three of them were out the door before she finished. She stacked the catechisms, straightened the chairs, and headed for the narthex. She glanced in at the broken window and noted that Roy had neatly patched it with cardboard and duct tape.

She would have a little time after the service while Jack finished up for the evening. She would look at the windows then. Maybe it would be easier to see patterns when it was dark out and the colors weren't getting in the way.

The service was short but engaging. The sermon series for Lent was the Seven Words from the cross, and tonight's word was "It is Finished". For a little while, she was able to forget the world around her, the disruption and chaos in her community.

All too soon, though, it came rushing back. She wished all of this were finished, the murderer caught, the ill feelings repaired. As the last people left for home, she moved back into the nave with a new determination.

She started methodically with the second window, the Baptism of Jesus. She used her thumbs and forefingers as a frame to help focus on one small section at a time. Nothing.

She moved on to the Good Shepherd. This time she saw it. It looked like two little hand towels on a rack, lost in the legs of the sheep. One of the towels had a lacey edge. Hmmm. She wrote "towels" in her notebook in the appropriate box and moved on to the Crucifixion.

After scanning the whole window and finding nothing there, she was about to move on, when she saw it out of the corner of her eye. The picture had a snake at the foot of the cross. That wasn't surprising. Many depictions of the crucifixion had a snake under the cross to symbolize Christ crushing the head of the Serpent in reference to Genesis 3:15. What was different was that it was coiled like a question mark and even had the dot underneath it. She wrote "question mark" in her notebook and moved on the next window.

"AAARRGH! Finding any hidden trrreasure?" said Jack in pirate-ese. He had sneaked up behind her again and she jumped.

"I swear you do that on purpose!" she said.

"Can you ever forgive me?" he smirked and kissed her.

"Oh, well, when you ask like that... OK." She smiled and kissed him back.

"Let's go home. It's after nine."

Maddy looked with surprise at her watch. She had been looking at the windows for over 45 minutes. "Yes, let's go home. I can show you what I found tomorrow." Jack put his arm around her as they headed out.

CHAPTER TEN

On Thursday morning, as Maddy enjoyed her morning decaf and worked an 'insanely hard' Sudoku puzzle, she thought about whom to talk to first. *Vernella*, she thought. Vernella Matthews was 92 years old, and legally blind from macular degeneration. But her mind was as sharp as a tack. She didn't get out much, but she loved visitors. She would remember who was involved in the rebuilding of the church.

Twenty minutes later she was ringing the doorbell of the old farmhouse. Vernella was an inspiration for elderly people everywhere. She still lived in the farmhouse that she built with her husband 70 years ago. When her daughter and son-in-law took over the management of the farm, they built a new house about 200 yards away, and when their son, now in his thirties, decided he wanted to work the farm, he lived with Vernella until he married so that Vernella wouldn't be alone. Vernella's husband Lloyd had himself lived to a ripe old age and passed away about 15 years ago. Nathaniel, the grandson, had married Joe Buchholz's daughter, Mary, and they had built a nice little three-bedroom ranch style on the other side of the property. Maddy reflected how most of the families were related somehow by blood or marriage. After three or four generations of family farming, there was bound to be a lot of intermarriage in the area. Anyway, Nate had worried about Vernella living alone, but she wouldn't leave her house. She knew every inch of the place, and now that she was nearly blind, that familiarity was important. Watching her move confidently about her home, you might not know she could only see shadows of light and dark. So instead, Nate and Mary, and their three-year old son and baby daughter ate dinner with "Great Gramma" two to three times a week, cooking in her kitchen, and leaving plenty of easily reheatable leftovers for her. The other days always saw either the kids or grandkids checking in to make sure she was OK, and doing little things to help, like cleaning up any dishes, vacuuming, or taking her laundry to be done at their houses.

Vernella opened the door, leaning on her white cane.

Maddy quickly introduced herself, knowing that Vernella couldn't see who it was. "Hello, Vernella. It's Madalyn Mitchell."

"Well, Madalyn, dear, come on in. What brings you out to the farm?" said Vernella, stepping back so that Maddy could enter. She led the way to the living room, only using her cane to find the edge of the doorway, and sat in her favorite easy chair.

"It's been too long since I visited, and I just wanted to sit and chat. I hope I'm not interrupting anything."

Vernella laughed. She didn't leave the house except for church and some holidays, which Maddy knew very well.

"Shall I make some tea?" offered Maddy.

"That would be lovely, dear. I like mine with cream and sugar. You know, during the depression we couldn't afford cream and sugar, and during the war, those luxuries were rationed. So many of my friends became so used to drinking their tea and coffee black, they never went back to cream and sugar, but not me! I savor every drop of sweet, creamy goodness and thank God for granting me such blessings that I can enjoy them."

That was the neatest thing about talking with Vernella. She told the most incredible stories. And now, elderly, blind, and living on a fixed income, she thanked God for her blessings. She had an entire dresser full of pictures—including many sepia-toned photos dating back to the twenties and thirties. Maddy had spent an afternoon looking through them one time, just admiring the clothes and hairstyles of the past, and experiencing the overall wonder of looking back into another time.

"So how old were you during the depression?" Maddy asked as she brought the tea into the living room and placed Vernella's cup on the end table next to her chair.

"Well, I graduated from high school in 1934, the middle of the depression. I had wanted to go to beauty school and become a hairdresser, but it cost $100 and there was no way my father could get that kind of money. So, I started knocking on doors, offering my services to cook, clean, and care for children. I earned two dollars a week."

Maddy sipped her tea, appreciating the way Vernella brought the past to life. "You were one of the founding members of St. Paul's, weren't you?" she asked.

"Yes, I suppose you could say that" said Vernella with a smile. "Actually, I was only about ten or eleven years old. My father and Mr. Johnson and our two families started the church in 1927. Our first pastor was a circuit rider, you know, a pastor that rode around to several churches. He came every six weeks. I was confirmed by him in 1929. But we were growing and soon we were able to call our own pastor. Things got tough during the depression. Toward the end we were paying the pastor with produce from our gardens and hens from our chicken coops. But he stuck it out with the rest of us and said the Lord would provide. And He has!"

"Some people may not have thought that when the church burned down," reflected Maddy. She sipped her tea and mentally patted herself on the back for steering the conversation toward the rebuilding of the church.

"Oh, no one couldn't say that after the insurance company paid for the entire rebuilding, including the windows!" said Vernella with spirit. "The church looks much like it did before, but now it's newer, with updated plumbing and electricity. And I do like the padded pews."

She smiled again, but suddenly stopped. "Excuse me, dear; I need to visit the facilities." And she got up and left the room.

Maddy was used to these interruptions. Vernella had diverticulitis which required frequent visits to the bathroom. She had suffered from it for as long as Maddy had known her, but she was determinedly cheerful, refusing to be embarrassed by that or her other infirmities. She always said that God gave her illness and infirmity to give those around her the opportunity to help her and to make her realize that in this life we are dependent on those who love us.

She returned shortly and said, "Now where were we? Oh, yes, the rebuilding of the church after that dreadful fire."

"Who was in charge of the rebuilding?" asked Maddy.

"Let's see, Stan Johnson and Roger McBride were trustees, George Olson was the congregation president, and I think Harold Arbuthnot was the head elder, but he's passed on. Pastor Shultz was the pastor then. He took a call to somewhere in Mississippi two years later."

"How about Harold Broomfield?" asked Maddy. "Was he involved?"

"Harold Broomfield? No, he was just a young fellow at the time, still in college if I remember correctly. No, he wasn't really involved with the church rebuilding, although he and that Zachariah Hendergast did seem to hit it off when he was home from college for the summer."

"Do you remember how it was decided that Hendergast would do the stained-glass windows?" asked Maddy.

Vernella thought for a minute, then said, "I remember there being a congregational meeting where we voted on things like what scenes would be in the windows along with what pews we wanted, what light fixtures, and so on. I think that it had already been decided that he would do them. I believe that the church council and board of trustees determined all the contractors."

Maddy made a mental note to question Stan Johnson and Roger McBride. George Olson was in an assisted living home, but he was Penny's dad, so it would be easy to visit him along with Penny sometime. That was three more people who might give her some answers.

"Did you ever hear anything about Mr. Hendergast blackmailing people for favors?" she asked.

Vernella laughed. "Oh, my, yes! Do you know he tried to blackmail me? You see, he found out about my diverticulitis and actually had the nerve to 'suggest' that I should hire him to do odd jobs around the house for $10 an hour. I know that may not seem like much now, but remember that minimum wage was less than $3 an hour back then. He wasn't very subtle, mind you, but he implied that if I didn't hire him and pay him that outrageous salary, that he would tell people about my diverticulitis. I just laughed and told him that not only did I have a son-in-law, daughter and grandkids to do things for me, but people already know about my condition. Why should I be ashamed of it? I was getting old, and things like that happen to old people." She chuckled quietly at the memory.

"He wasn't very happy about it, but what could he do? Complain to the sheriff that I wouldn't acquiesce to his blackmail? 'Course, some people did complain to the sheriff about his trying to blackmail them, but he wouldn't do anything. Said it wasn't really a crime because he wasn't asking for money outright. I never believed that for a minute. Now that I think about it, maybe Zachariah was blackmailing him to look the other way. He sure did pretty much as he pleased around town. Hmmm."

Maddy was startled. That didn't sound like Joe. "Joe Buchholz let him get away with blackmail when he knew about it and people had complained?" she asked incredulously.

"Oh, my, no. That was old Sheriff Madsen. He was old and just wanted to retire, which he did about three to four years later. Then he died of prostate cancer the next year. Kind of sad." Vernella sipped her tea and rocked her chair.

"Well, enough about the past. How have you been? Is Mark coming home for Easter?"

"Yes, he is," said Maddy, "he'll be home for Good Friday, too. He will have to be back to class Monday morning, though."

They chatted for several minutes more, but Vernella was looking tired. Maddy made her excuses and left so that Vernella could lie down for a nap.

Driving back to town, she thought about what she'd learned. It seemed Zachariah Hendergast had attempted blackmailing practically everyone in town. That would certainly stir up a lot of hard feelings collectively, but so far as she knew, none of the secrets were incriminating enough to spur someone to murder, or were they? His source of blackmail-worthy information seemed to be primarily the

Pharmacy where he worked part time, and the 'secrets' seemed to be mainly health and medical issues. If he found out about something worse than chronic diarrhea, like a sexually transmitted disease or an abortion, something that would tear apart a marriage or a family, it might be a motive for murder. She'd also learned that his demands included well-paid jobs. The replacement of the stained-glass windows had certainly been a well-paid job. What if he blackmailed someone at the church to be sure he got the job?

Maddy snapped out of her reverie with the realization that there were flashing lights behind her. She pulled her little grey Volkswagon Golf over onto the shoulder and rolled down her window. With a sigh of relief, she saw that it was Joe Buchholz. She had no idea what she'd done, so she plastered on a smile and reached for her registration.

"Maddy, do realize you just blew through the stop sign back there?"

Maddy's jaw dropped. "I... I... I'm sorry. I guess my mind was elsewhere." Her face turned red with embarrassment, and she handed her registration and license through the window.

Joe's mouth flattened into a look of combined amusement and frustration. "I'm going to let you go with a warning. But you pay attention to your driving! You know how you get distracted when your mind is wandering." He waved away the license and registration. "Now you get yourself safely home to Jack and don't run anymore stop signs!"

Maddy nodded repeatedly during the lecture, feeling like the 'Bobble-head Luther' in Jack's study. "I will! I mean, I won't. ... Thank you" she added sheepishly.

She wasn't sure if it was appropriate to ask him about the murder, having just been pulled over for running a stop sign, but she jumped in anyway, not wanting to lose the opportunity. "Um, have you made any progress on the murder investigation?" she asked.

Joe pursed his lips, but then decided to answer. "Actually... no. Plenty of gossip about his blackmailing activities in the past, but no leads to his murder in the present. Frankly, I'm amazed at what he got away with. It's hard to believe that Sheriff Madsen didn't charge him with anything. Apparently, some people complained, but he just didn't do anything." He shook his head in disbelief.

"Maybe Hendergast was blackmailing him, too," suggested Maddy.

Joe looked thoughtful but didn't comment.

"Did you learn anything from the autopsy?" asked Maddy.

Joe sighed. "Not really. We already knew he was strangled with some type of belt or strap. So, there were no fingerprints or hand marks."

"Doesn't that mean the murderer needed to be someone strong?"

"Not necessarily. Using a strap both narrows the compression site and distributes it around the neck. It also reduces the amount of force needed to occlude the carotid artery…", Joe stopped himself abruptly. "I really shouldn't be talking about this with you. Don't you go getting involved! It could be dangerous!"

Maddy nodded contritely. "Thank you for letting me off with a warning. I'll be more careful!"

While Joe left, she calmed herself with a little prayer. Then she looked carefully over her shoulder, signaled, and pulled back onto the road.

"Jack, I got pulled over by Joe today. I accidently ran a stop sign out by county road 17. He let me off with a warning, but I figured he'd tell you sooner or later, and I'd rather you heard it from me."

Jack looked up from his tuna casserole. "What took you out there?" *How like Jack,* she thought, *to not dwell on the infraction.* He knew she was mortified and would be extra careful from now on.

"I was visiting Vernella," she answered. She told him what she'd learned.

"Hmmm," said Jack thoughtfully, "I'm going to be seeing Roger today about getting the widow repaired. I'll ask him what he remembers about how the job was assigned." He finished up his lunch and stood up. Maddy picked up the dishes and put them in the sink.

"I think I'll go visit Stan, then, after I clean up." she said.

Jack kissed her goodbye and headed back over to the church. Cleaning up after lunch took less than ten minutes. She didn't want to visit the Johnsons until later in the afternoon. It was planting season and he would probably be out in the fields until later. She sat down at her computer to check her e-mail. To her delight, there were e-mails from each of her children.

To: channelingkatie@cable.com

From: themathguy@ui.edu

Subject: Easter

Hi, Mom!

Can't wait 4 Easter weekend! Can I bring a friend? We should arrive about 2ish on Friday.

Love ya,

Mark

She smiled and replied that, of course, he could bring a friend. She'd make up the other twin bed in his room. The twin beds had originally been Martha's and Joanna's. When they'd moved to Iowa, and a larger house, they got their own rooms with a full size bed for Martha, and Joanna kept the twin beds in her room so her friends could stay over. When Martha went to college, Joanna co-opted her room, Mark got the matching twin beds, and his smaller youth bed was donated to the Goodwill, making room for Maddy to finally get an office/sewing room. Now Joanna's room was a guest room, but Mark still had his room for summers and holidays.

To: channelingkatie@cable.com

From: adaspira@mit.edu

Subject: Easter plans

Hi, Mom!

I know I was going to come home for Easter, but I'm so busy getting ready for summer internship that I think I'll stay here. I had put off getting plane tickets and now they'd cost a fortune anyway, unless I used frequent flyer miles. I'll visit between Spring and Summer semesters, around the end of May. I'll be much less stressed then. Don't worry. I won't be alone—Seamus is taking me out for brunch.

Talk to you later.

Love,

Joanna

Maddy sighed. She should have expected that. Joanna was so busy as a graduate student. Or maybe she just didn't want to be away from her new heartthrob. Maddy paused to consider. If that were the real reason, it's too bad she didn't bring him along.

She did want to meet Seamus. Oh, well. It would be nice to see her in May. She replied back:

To: adaspira@mit.edu

From: channelingkatie@cable.com wrote:

Subject: Re: Easter

Joanna,

I fully understand, but I will miss you! I will sure enjoy seeing you in May. Bring Seamus with you, if you can. We'd love to meet him! You'll be able to see your new niece or nephew then, too.

Love,

Mom

She moved on to the last e-mail.

To: channelingkatie@cable.com

From: theonlyolnies@nbx.com

Subject: Stressed and Tired

Mom,

Now I know why you and Dad were always so tired after Easter! Harlan is introducing Easter Vigil to the congregation this year, so that's five services during Holy Week, counting Palm Sunday. He's got the Maundy Thursday, Good Friday, and Easter Vigil sermons done, but still needs to work out the details for the special services. Some of the people in the congregation are throwing a fit, saying the Easter Vigil is 'too Catholic', but others are really looking forward to it. I hope it doesn't rain so we can have the candle lighting outdoors before processing into the church. Then again, remembering what happened when the youth bonfire last summer got out of control and nearly burned the church down, maybe just lighting the candle in the narthex would be better. I just hope our little one can wait until after Easter. He or she isn't due for another 2 to 3 weeks, but someone told me that the first one can come early.

I'm getting so tired these days, I just spend most afternoons with my feet up, trying to take down the swelling in my feet. Thanks for the suggestion about the little pillow under the stomach! I'm sleeping better now, even if Harlan isn't. The house is a wreck, but Harlan is so nice about it. He even did a load of blacks yesterday because he was out of clerical collars to wear, and didn't say a word to me about it. I feel so guilty because he's so busy right now. All I want to do some days is just sit in the rocking chair and rock. I tell myself I'm practicing for when the baby is born. Soon, Easter will be past and then the baby will come. Pray for us!

Love,

Martha

Maddy felt a surge of excitement thinking again of their first grandchild. Martha and Harlan had decided they didn't want to know the sex of the baby until it was born, so she didn't know if they were getting a grandson or a granddaughter. Not that it mattered; it just made it harder to buy baby clothes and toys ahead of time. Maddy caught herself and laughed. How silly! When Martha was born, ultrasound wasn't available and when she was expecting Joanna, they'd gotten an ultrasound, but the technician mistakenly told them they were having a boy. Joanna had worn some of the blue onesies, little coveralls, and baseball caps that had been given to them at the baby shower, but Maddy had always dressed them up with bows on her head and ruffley socks and shirts, so she looked like a girl. It hadn't helped that she had been born completely bald. Maddy got lost in thought wondering what their first grandchild would be like. She didn't even know what names they had picked out. Martha said that they kept changing their minds, so they weren't going to tell anyone until the birth certificate was completed. With a last name like Olnie, they wanted something that wasn't too hard to pronounce and didn't sound silly. At least it was unique. Their joke was that they were the only Olnies, hence her e-mail address.

Maddy sighed contentedly, then looked at the clock. It was after two already. She browsed the internet looking for a decent looking toaster for Martha. She finally found a nice one with one long, wide slot that would accommodate wide slices of bread and thick bagels. It got generally good reviews, so she typed in her credit card information, put Martha and Harlan's address in the 'send to' page, and added a note saying, "Happy Easter, from Mom & Dad." She clicked the finalize button, closed the browser, locked her computer, and got up. She still had some time before she wanted to head out to the Johnson farm, so she headed for the Community Health Center instead.

"Hi!" said Penny, looking up from her computer. "What's up?"

Maddy sat down with a sigh. "Got a few minutes? I know I shouldn't bug you at work, but this is really weighing on me."

Penny saved her work and turned toward Maddy. "Of course! What's wrong? Is it one of the kids? Are Martha and the baby OK?"

"Oh, no, they're fine. It's this murder," said Maddy, seriously. She outlined her thoughts from the night before, how she felt like her life had been altered, that the murder had intruded and taken something away from their community. "I've got to find out who did it so I can stop wondering which one of my friends is a murderer."

"Oh, come on! I don't really think it's one of our friends. I mean, they might get angry or catty, but no one we know would actually kill someone. Besides, finding the killer is a job best left to the Sheriff and his deputies. They know what they're doing."

"I'm not saying they don't," said Maddy quickly. "But they still don't have any leads, and they have other things to do besides look at stained-glass windows."

"Oh, right. And you have all the time in the world!" said Penny sarcastically.

"Well, that's why I want you to help. And I've been thinking about who it could be and who it couldn't. It has to be someone in town, someone who knew Hendergast thirty years ago. So it's going to be someone our age or older. It's also probably someone in the church, because of the windows. Hendergast made the windows, and someone deliberately broke one of them. That narrows it down quite a bit, and, much as I hate to think about it, it's probably someone we know, even someone we're friends with." Maddy paused and looked meaningfully at Penny, who was nodding.

"OK. I can't argue with that," she finally admitted. "So, where do we start?"

"Well, as you know, I've already started with the windows." She told Penny about the picture of the towels in the Good Shepherd window that she'd found the night before. "And I've gotten together a list of people to talk to." She told her about her conversation with Vernella and her plans to talk to Stan that afternoon.

"That sounds like a good start. We can certainly talk to Dad this week sometime. I don't know how much time I'll have to talk to people, but I can help look at windows, and I'll have more time after the health fair." Penny stopped and thought for a minute. "We'll probably see quite a few people at the fair, but I don't know if we'll have much time to really talk to them."

"That's OK. We can just keep our ears open at the fair. People certainly seem to be willing to talk about Hendergast, and they don't seem to be holding anything back," said Maddy wryly.

"Isn't that encouraging gossip?" asked Penny.

Maddy thought for a minute. "Yes, it is. But I think it's for a good cause. It's not like we're going to repeat any of it." She paused, feeling guilty. "I just can't think of another way to get information."

Penny nodded again. "You're probably right."

"Well, I think I'll head out to Stan and Janet's. They should be back to the house by now. And I should let you get back to work." Maddy picked up her purse and keys.

"Just let me know what you want me to do," said Penny. Maddy waved her thanks and headed out the door.

Janet answered the door in jeans, sweatshirt, and stocking feet. Her dark blond hair was pulled back in a rough ponytail and her muddy shoes next to the door indicated that she'd recently come in from outdoors. She had that healthy glow of people who spend a lot of time outdoors. "Hi, Janet! Is Stan around?"

"Hardly!" answered Janet. "He's behind on the planting because of all the rain. He probably won't come in until it's too dark to steer the tractor. I just finished tilling the garden and outlining the rows."

"Oh," said Maddy. "I was just hoping to ask him some questions. I don't want to take up your time if you're busy."

"Nonsense. I'm done for today. I wasn't planning to start planting until next week. It's too early, even for peas and beans. Come in and have some coffee." Janet motioned Maddy into the house. "I can't believe you drove all the way out here just to ask a couple questions."

"Well, it's something that's got my curiosity up, and I fancied a little drive. Maybe you can help me." She sat on the sofa while Janet brought in two cups of coffee and then a creamer and sugar bowl. Maddy immediately spooned sugar and instant creamer into her cup and stirred.

"Sure, if I can," said Janet. "What's on your mind?"

"Well, I was wondering about the rebuilding of the church, and how they decided who would replace the stained-glass windows," Maddy began.

"I'm pretty sure Zachariah Hendergast did them," said Janet, "but I don't remember much about the rebuilding. That was not too long after we were married, and I was pregnant with Brian. I had terrible morning sickness with him and spent most of my time at home. We were the last couple married in the old church before it burned down. Stan was very busy with the rebuilding. He was the youngest trustee at the time. Of course, he's always been very involved at church. He really threw himself into the service of the church after Claire died."

"Claire was his first wife?" asked Maddy. She realized that Janet wasn't going to be much help recalling what happened during the church rebuilding, but she found that she was comfortable talking to her and was enjoying the conversation.

"Yes. It was so sad when she died. She was so young, and she and Stan had been high-school sweethearts. She was diagnosed with cancer the year after they were married, and she died 18 months after that. It was ovarian cancer, I think. The chemotherapy was so hard on her. She lost all her hair and was tired all the time. Then she had a stroke and was in the nursing home for several months. But she did seem to be recovering from the stroke, and it seemed like the cancer was responding to the chemotherapy and they let her go home. Then, all of a sudden, she was gone. Stan was devastated. We became close toward the end of Claire's illness, while she was recovering from her stroke. Nothing inappropriate, mind you," she added quickly, "we were friends, and he needed a friend. Then Claire came home from the nursing home, and he was trying to care for her, look after his mother, and work the farm all at the same time. He was exhausted."

She paused to sip her coffee. "Then she died, and he was so lost. We spent more and more time together, and… just… fell in love. We got married about six months later." She smiled with that faraway look people get when thinking of good memories.

"Did you go to high school with Stan and Claire?" Maddy asked.

"No, we knew each other from youth group. I grew up in Wheatonville and graduated just before they closed the school and started busing the kids here to Marshallhaven."

Wheatonville was one of the tiny rural towns supported by the farmers. Like so many small towns, it had been dwindling for decades until there wasn't much left but a few homes, a post office, and an International Harvester dealer. Even the Catholic Church had closed its doors several years ago when their priest retired, and they'd joined with the parish in Marshallhaven. The Lutheran church in Wheatonville, St Mark's, had been part of a dual parish with St. Paul's in Marshallhaven, but had closed their doors in the 1970s, being unable to afford the upkeep on the church building. The little church had been bought by a young artistic couple who had converted it into a luxurious home and studio. Maddy was glad that Jack did not have to serve a dual parish. His first call had been to a dual parish and he was always exhausted, going back and forth and conducting twice as many services, bible studies, confirmation classes, etc.

"Speaking of lasts, I was in the last graduating class, and I was also the last Miss Wheatonville," continued Janet.

"Really! I guess that's something to tell your children," said Maddy.

Janet giggled. "If you must know, there were only four contestants, and the other three became runners up by default. It was a Junior Miss pageant, you know, for high school girls. They hadn't had a pageant for several years and my three friends and I and our Mothers decided to put on one more pageant before the school closed. It was a lot of fun going to the parades and events around the state. Of course, I didn't even make runner up at state."

Maddy found herself wondering why she hadn't gotten to know Janet better. She was easy to talk to. She found herself telling Janet how she had met Jack at college when he was in his senior year of pre-sem. They'd gotten married the summer before he started seminary and they had struggled to get through seminary while she finished up her nursing degree. Despite the hardships, it had been an idyllic time. Newly married and happy, they had lived in a tiny studio apartment in Springfield, Illinois, living on food from the seminary food co-op and dreaming of their future. Maddy and Janet both talked about their children, and before she knew it, it was almost suppertime. "I've really got to go," said Maddy, "but I've really enjoyed talking to you. See you Sunday!"

CHAPTER ELEVEN

Friday was set-up day for the Health Fair, and as Maddy planned to spend most of the day helping Penny, she wanted to at least start her laundry and clean the bathroom before she had to meet Penny at 9:00. She got a load of towels washing, sat down to finish her cup of coffee from breakfast, and glanced at the paper. Oh, no. She should have expected it, but still.

MYSTERIOUS VANDAL DESTROYS STAINED-GLASS jumped from the front page. Hmmm. Her earlier imagined headline hadn't been that far off. The article continued—

"Sheriff Buchholz is investigating a case of mysterious vandalism to a stained-glass window at St. Paul Lutheran Church. Roy Zabel, church trustee, discovered the breakage and reported the crime to the sheriff's office on Monday morning. The instrument of breakage was a baseball, but Pastor Jack Mitchell suspects the incident is more sinister than a simple schoolboy accident. He noted that the ball appeared to be new, and a ball hit through the window by accident would be expected to show a certain amount of wear and tear. "It looks to me like the window was broken first and the ball thrown through the hole to make it look like an accident," said Madalyn Mitchell, wife of Pastor Mitchell. Sheriff Buchholz agreed, noting that the window was broken in such a way to suggest multiple impacts. He has asked if anyone saw anything unusual around St. Paul's on Sunday night to please contact the sheriff's office at 555-4321."

Not too bad, if a bit sensationalistic, thought Maddy. "A case of mysterious vandalism" and "crime" seemed to be a bit overboard, but technically it was a crime. Lucien didn't have any other crime to report, so she couldn't fault him for playing it up a little. True to his word, he'd quoted her exactly. She wondered how the vandal, who was probably also the murderer, would respond. Would this make him (or her?) lie low and not risk breaking any more windows? Or would he feel pressured to try to break more as quickly as possible? Would he make a mistake, do something rash that would reveal his identity? Would he be more dangerous now?

Maddy glanced at the next article. RIVER RISING SLOWS. "The Army Corps of Engineers released its latest predictions yesterday, stating that the river is still rising, but that the rate of increase has slowed. Since the building of the sandbag wall downtown by a crew of volunteers last Monday, the river has risen an additional eighteen inches. Current projections have the water cresting at thirty-seven feet, six feet above flood stage."

Maddy did a quick calculation in her head. That would be another three feet plus the foot and a half since Monday, which would be well contained by the sandbag wall. So far so good. She started to glance back at the article when the washer finished its spin cycle. Thinking of how much she needed to do, Maddy dropped the paper back onto the table.

Two hours later found her sitting on an incredibly uncomfortable folding chair in a corner while Penny and the other volunteers set up tables, chairs, portable cooking stations, and large displays with temperature charts and pictures of food in various stages of preparation. She was busy helping Penny by calling to remind all the volunteers when to show up for their shifts. Most were spending only a couple hours volunteering at the fair except for those giving cooking demonstrations, who had agreed to spend the whole six hours there. The food pictures and the samples stations were starting to make her hungry. She was on her own for lunch because Jack had his monthly ministerial association meeting at noon. Penny was too busy to stop for lunch so she offered to get a couple sandwiches from Sarah's Bakery and bring them back to the community center.

The bakery was busier on Fridays than on Tuesdays and she waited in line for about 10 minutes before reaching the counter. Sarah herself was working the takeout line, frowning as usual. Maddy smiled her friendliest smile and ordered two turkey club sandwiches and reached into her purse for her wallet.

"You'll have to wait a bit, Donna's cutting some more turkey," said Sarah, gruffly.

"That's no problem," said Maddy smiling again. She turned to let someone behind her be helped while she was waiting, but she was the last in line.

She turned back to Sarah. "I'm sorry for your loss," she said.

"Whaddhya mean?" said Sarah with surprise.

"I'm sorry. I was given to understand that you and Zachariah Hendergast had been close."

Sarah looked at her sourly. "Is that what you heard?" Then suddenly she gave a harsh bark of a laugh. "I'm sorry, I know you're just bein' nice, and all. Yeah, we were 'close', and stupid me, I thought it meant something to him. When he just up an' left without a word to me, I kept thinking he was coming back. It wasn't too long before I realized that he was never coming back, he didn't love me, and that old saying about gettin' the milk for free was all too true." She sighed.

"I'm sorry. That must have really hurt," said Maddy, sympathetically.

"Yeah, it did. But what hurt more was all the gossiping and people looking at me when they thought I wasn't looking. I know what everyone thought and said about me, and still do. That I'm some kind of evil sinner. When he was found dead, any feelings I'd had for him were long dead, too, but it sure brought up all the old gossip. I thought that if I cleaned up my life, they'd be a little nicer to me."

Donna brought a tray of sliced turkey from the back room and slid it into the empty slot in the sandwich making line. Sarah started making the sandwiches, swiping the mayonnaise knife and slapping the slices down with somewhat greater than necessary vigor. "Some of the younger people in town that don't know my past, they're nice to me. You've always been nice to me. I even thought about going back to church when you and your husband came. I was confirmed at St. Paul's, you know. But the thought of all those self-righteous, stuck-up people sitting in their pews looking down their noses at me… you know what I mean?"

"Yes," said Maddy, "sinners, every one of them."

Sarah looked completely startled. She froze momentarily, then continued assembling the sandwich with that jerky motion that indicates a failed attempt to look natural. That had obviously not been the response she'd expected. "All *them* good people? None of them ever 'lived in sin', or smoked pot, or, or,…" Sarah stopped for lack of words.

"That doesn't mean they haven't sinned in other ways. Church is for sinners, and we all qualify. Church is where we all get forgiveness."

Sarah looked away, a brief succession of expressions flitting across her face: incredulity, suspicion, disdain, and a just little hint of hope. She handed over the sandwiches and accepted payment without a word. Maddy said thank you and was about to turn away, when Sarah muttered, almost too low to hear, "Could I sit with you?" Maddy leaned in a little closer over the glass display case and said kindly, "I'll save a spot for you," and left.

By 2:30 they were done setting up. "I'm going to visit Dad. Would you like to come?" asked Penny. George Olson had moved to the assisted living apartments last year. He was in his seventies and his arthritis had gotten too bad for him to do things around the house. Penny's mother, Mary, had died over ten years ago, and he was finally able to let go of the house they'd shared for so long. It was a nice day, so Maddy and Penny walked the six blocks to the Lutherhaven Assisted Living complex. George lived in one of the little cottages on the outskirts where someone would come in daily to check on him and do light housekeeping. He could cook in the little kitchen if he wanted, or join the other retirees in the main building's dining hall if he didn't want to cook and clean up. He was sitting in his favorite chair—a brown leather Lazy Boy that Penny had given him for Christmas a few years ago—watching game shows on television when they arrived.

"Come in, Come in!" he said, delighted to have visitors. "Can I get you something to drink?"

"Now, Dad, you just sit down. I can get us something," said Penny. "What would you like?" she asked Maddy.

"Oh, water's fine." Maddy sat down on the faded grey couch as George turned the sound off on the television, leaving the contestants animated but silent. His little apartment was clean but cluttered. Pictures of George proudly holding a twenty-pound Northern Pike, George and Mary on their wedding day, and Penny and Mary sitting next to a Christmas tree wearing seventies style clothing all hung on the wall next to the television. Books and magazines were stacked next to an empty milk glass on the side table within easy reach of the lazyboy. A plate with crumbs on it sat on the floor next to George's left foot, clearly more convenient than the coffee table which was far enough away to accommodate the chair's extended footrest and George's slippered feet. From the faint lingering odor, Maddy guessed that his lunch sandwich had been ham and cheese with mustard.

"So what brings two lovely young ladies to my house this fine spring day?" he asked with a twinkle in his eye.

"Oh, just thought we'd come for a visit. We just finished setting up for the health fair."

"Oh, yes, the health fair! I'll have to come check that out. Will you be taking blood pressures again?"

"Mmm-hmmm. Just like always." Maddy accepted a glass of water from Penny, who sat down next to her. "Do you remember when the church was rebuilt? What can you tell me about that process?" asked Maddy setting her glass on the coffee table.

George sipped his coffee and said, "Oh, I remember, all right. I was congregation president at the time. It was pretty involved. Fortunately we had insurance. But we had to account for every aspect of the rebuilding and keep the insurance company up to date on our progress. It really worked out well. The church had been wanting to remodel and build a parish hall, and they got pretty much everything they wanted in the rebuilding. See, before, the parish hall was in the basement, and it was hard for the older people to get up and down the stairs. And there were some pretty steep steps up to the front door of the church, too. Now everything's at ground level. Much better for us old folks. It's so hard when you get old. You don't feel old inside, but everything is just so much harder to do." He sighed and took another sip of his coffee, dripping a small amount on his sweater vest. He dabbed at it halfheartedly with the napkin Penny had handed him with his coffee.

"Don't worry about it Dad, I'll wash it out later," said Penny firmly.

George beamed at Maddy. "She takes such good care of me. I don't know what I'd do without her."

"She certainly does," agreed Maddy. "So, what about the stained-glass windows? Did the insurance really pay for them?"

"Oh, yes. The original windows had been separately insured, in case of breakage, so there was no question about replacing them. It was just a matter of finding someone to do them. Zachariah Hendergast did a good job, but he wasn't the only one considered. There were two glaziers in Des Moines that bid for the job as well."

"Was Hendergast's bid the lowest one?" Penny asked in surprise.

"No, actually it was the highest. But the church council decided that using a local artist would keep the money local and help support the town economy. His bid was just within the highest amount that the insurance company would pay, so they voted to hire him."

"Was there any dispute about it, or was the decision to use Hendergast pretty much a consensus?" asked Maddy.

"Well, as I recall, once Stan and Roger outlined the situation, it seemed like everyone agreed that there was no reason not to hire him." Maddy wasn't sure if that was consensus or not, but didn't want to seem too obvious.

They finished their drinks, chatted about the weather and whether or not the downtown would get flooded out, and then took their leave.

As they walked back toward their cars, Penny asked, "What was that about consensus?"

"Just an idea I had, that maybe the commission for the windows was a payoff for some of Hendergast's blackmail," answered Maddy.

"Who would he have blackmailed? The whole council?"

"I don't know. It was just an idea," said Maddy thoughtfully.

That evening at dinner she remembered that she hadn't told Jack about what she'd found in the windows. The set up for the Health Fair had been completed around two, so she had done some more window gazing and had what she thought might be two more anomalies. She decided to wait until they'd eaten and then show him the grid in her notebook.

"I talked to Roger yesterday," he was saying, taking a large bite of lasagna. "He said he couldn't remember who brought up the suggestion to have Hendergast do the stained-glass, but the council talked it over and it was between him and a larger company in Des Moines. He said that after they saw the quality of his work, and considered that it would keep the money local, they were all for it, even though he was asking more than the Des Moines company. After all, the insurance was going to cover it."

Maddy picked Andante out of her chair and put her on the floor. "Hmmm. So it didn't seem like one person was really pushing for him more than the others?" she asked.

"Not to hear Roger tell it," said Jack. "Why?"

"Well, I was just wondering if Zachariah might have used leverage over one of the council members to get the job at such a high price." said Maddy.

"Doesn't seem that way," answered Jack.

"No, that's pretty much what George said, too," said Maddy.

"So, let's see what you've got with the windows," said Jack. Maddy opened her notebook and showed him her grid.

Nativity	Baptism of Jesus	Good Shepherd	Crucifixion	Resurrection
Candy Canes		Towels	Question Mark	*broken*
Creation	Temptation of Adam & Eve	Noah's Ark	Parting the Red Sea	Fall of Jericho
Horse		Spray Bottle	Wheat? Grain?	Anvil

"Well, I have to admit that you're on to something here. But it's all nonsense. It doesn't mean anything," said Jack.

"I know, but maybe when I find the rest, it'll make sense," she said.

"Which window was broken, again?" asked Jack.

"The Resurrection," said Maddy, pointing to the chart.

"So, how do you know the anomaly on that window hasn't been damaged?" he asked. Maddy looked at him. He'd just voiced the thought she had in the back of her mind since last Monday.

"That's exactly what I think," said Maddy pointedly. She watched the wheels turning in Jack's head as he looked again at the notebook.

Chapter Twelve

"So, you see, if your potato salad sits out at room temperature more than four hours, pathogenic bacteria that are frequently found on potatoes can grow in the salad and make you sick." Penny was explaining one of the posters outlining the six things that food pathogens need to grow. "Most bad bugs need a certain amount of time to produce enough bacteria or toxin to make you sick."

He didn't seem to understand. "But my wife makes her potato salad with egg-free salad dressing, not mayonnaise," he said. "and that means it's safe to leave out, right?"

Penny took a deep breath and started over. The Health Fair was a big success. It was only 11:30 and they'd been swamped. Maddy was glad she was just taking blood pressures. She was seated at the end of a small rectangular table with an armed chair set facing her across the corner.

"Your blood pressure is 120 over 90—just fine." She took the cuff off an elderly woman who looked like she would outlive Maddy herself and turned to the next person in line. A middle-aged gentleman sat down and rolled up his sleeve.

"I know it's gonna be high. I just can't remember to take my medicine since Alma passed on." He rolled up his sleeve and Maddy snugged the cuff around his upper arm, placed the bell of her stethoscope inside the crook of his elbow, and began inflating the cuff. She then let the air our slowly, listening for the heart beat that would tell her the systole and diastole—when the pressure is highest, when the heart pumps, and when the pressure is lowest, between beats.

Maddy smiled sympathetically as she removed the cuff. "Oh, my, its 160 over 120. When was the last time you had a checkup with your doctor?"

"Oh, I can't rightly recall," he said slowly.

"Well, you need to see your doctor this week. You don't want to have a stroke," she said, seriously.

"If you think so, I'll give her a call on Monday." He smiled and patted her hand. "You're awfully nice. Just like my doctor! Such a pretty young thing. Hard to believe she's a doctor. You take care, now." Maddy sometimes wasn't sure if the elderly men were just being polite or were hitting on her. She shook her head.

"I want to get my pressure taken from the pretty nurse at the second table!" said a voice.

Maddy looked up and then sighed. "Jack, your blood pressure is just fine."

"I'm not so sure. I think it's gone up just watching you."

Maddy laughed. "I don't suppose you would like to bring me some lunch. With this crowd I don't think I'll be able to get away."

"Sure thing. What do you want?"

"Ham and cheese sub with lots of mustard and extra olives."

"Coming right up" he said and was out the door. In no time he was back, and laid out the sandwiches, chips, and drinks on the back side of her table.

"So how was your morning?" she asked Jack as she took the stethoscope out of her ears and rubbed them gently. *Maybe she should get some of those soft rubber ear pieces,* she thought. She unwrapped her sub halfway, lifted the edge to inspect the contents, then took a large, satisfying bite.

"Great!" said Jack as he popped open his little bag of chips. "There's no Bible study or Sunday school tomorrow because it's Palm Sunday, so I put the finishing touches on my sermon and made sure the palms and the gifts for the 8th graders who are getting confirmed are ready." He unwrapped his sandwich, peeled back the top slice of bread, and squeezed two packages of mayonnaise and one package of mustard onto the layered cold cuts, while Maddy looked on disapprovingly. He really didn't need all that mayonnaise, but maybe now wasn't a good time to say anything. Jack continued, "I'll meet with the confirmands and their parents this afternoon, and then I'll just need to go over my sermon once or twice after supper." He bit into his sandwich, chewed, swallowed, and then licked the back side of the sandwich, catching a blob of mayo that threatened to escape.

"I'll bet the kids are pretty nervous," said Maddy.

"Oh, they'll be fine. They know all the questions by heart, and I'll prompt them if they stumble," said Jack.

They chewed in contented silence for a bit, watching the fairgoers wandering among the booths, picking up pamphlets and freebies. It wasn't long before Jack was wadding up the wrappers and chip bag and stuffing them into the sack for disposal. "Oh, by the way, Allegro threw up on the carpet. I cleaned up most of it, but there's a stain."

"Was it a hairball or did she throw up her food?"

"Just a hairball. Well, I'll see you later." He gathered up the trash from their lunch, took Maddy's bag of chips that she had wordlessly pushed over to his side, kissed her, and left.

She turned back to the milling throng with a smile to indicate that she was again open for business. She saw Lenny Carlisle making his way among the tables and heading her way.

"Would you like your blood pressure taken?" she called, getting his attention.

He stopped and looked like he wasn't much interested, then said, "Why not?", sat down and rolled up his sleeve of his grey plaid flannel shirt.

"Terrible thing about this murder," she said conversationally while she fitted the cuff on his upper arm, "and the sheriff's department doesn't seem to be any closer to finding out who killed him."

"Hmmm," he said, non-commitally.

"Oh, that's right, I heard you didn't like Zachariah Hendergast", she said casually.

"What? Oh, well, no I didn't back when I knew him. But nobody deserves to be murdered. It just ain't right." At last, she had gotten a real response. She started inflating the cuff.

"Well, whoever it was, must have really held a grudge," she said casually.

Lenny looked at her. "You're not thinking it was me, are you? I guess if you didn't know any better, you might think that. I was pretty mad at him at one time. But it doesn't matter now. Funny enough, I was so mad that people would find out, but I wasn't about to give in to his demands. He wanted me to give him all the free scrap metal he wanted from the junk yard for those monstrosities he called his 'sculpture', can you believe it? He found out that my daughter Lizzie, you never met her, she's Sandra's younger sister; she lives up in Chicago now, well she got pregnant and was afraid to tell me, and her boyfriend drove her into Des Moines to get an abortion. Well, I found out anyway, because she got an infection and had to be treated by Doctor Murphy. I guess that's how Hendergast found out. I was so devastated for my little girl, and for my lost grandchild. I told her I loved her no matter what, and you know, it brought us closer together. Anyway, after that, I didn't really care if people found out, and when they did, our friends were still our friends. Funny how things work out, isn't it?"

Maddy agreed and removed the cuff.

"So, how am I doin'?" he asked.

"Your blood pressure is just fine," she said and smiled. "You have a nice day and enjoy the rest of the Health Fair."

"I will. Did you know they're cooking hamburgers over there to show you how to tell when it's cooked enough? They're even handing out free thermometers! I got to get me one of those. Burke Anderson ate a rare hamburger last year and got the sh.., um, the runs real bad. Said he couldn't wear nothing but his PJs 'cause he had to go to the bathroom so often." With one hand, he adjusted his comb over, which had begun to slip sideways, and off he went to the hamburger station.

Maddy sighed. There was one more suspect off the list due to lack of motive. So many people despised Zachariah Hendergast that one would think there would be plenty of motives. But it seemed that people had either moved on or never had that strong a personal motive to begin with. Thirty years was a long time, and as the saying goes, time heals all wounds. But someone hadn't moved on. Someone still hated him enough to kill him, even thirty years later.

CHAPTER THIRTEEN

Maddy looked out the kitchen window as she washed up the few supper dishes. The wind was picking up and black storm clouds were coming in from the southwest.

"Looks like we're in for a storm," she said to Jack.

"Looks like it. Let's go over my sermon quick and come home. It looks like it's going to be a great night for snuggling," he said with a grin.

As they walked over to the church, they saw Roy mowing the lawn, trying to finish up before the storm hit. They waved to him and went into the back door to Jack's study.

Forty-five minutes later, as they came out again, the storm was in full swing. Pouring rain, thunder, lightning, and stiff winds propelling them across the parking lot. Neither of them had thought to bring an umbrella and Maddy wanted nothing more than to get indoors and into something dry and warm. She had turned her head slightly to keep her whipping hair out of her eyes when she spotted the riding lawn mower sitting in the middle of the side lawn. It wasn't like Roy to forget to put it away, especially in bad weather. She pulled on Jack's arm and motioned toward the lawn mower. He looked as surprised as Maddy, and they both headed over to get a closer look.

There was no sign of Roy. Jack started up the mower and was moving it back to the shed and Maddy was running ahead to open the shed door, when they both heard the sound of breaking glass coming from the far side of the church. 'What now?' they mouthed to each other and, bent into the wind, made their way around the corner. Roy was face down in the grass with a huge tree branch lying beside him, and another branch was protruding from one of the stained-glass windows.

Maddy rushed over to Roy and felt for a pulse. "His pulse is steady and he's breathing," she bawled to Jack over the noise of the storm.

"I'll stay here with him, you go call 9-1-1," he yelled back. Maddy nodded and ran back to the study door. Once the ambulance was on its way, she went back outside to wait with Jack. He held his jacket over Roy to keep the rain out of his face and Maddy started massaging his wrists and gently slapping his cheeks. He moaned softly just as the ambulance arrived. Maddy was both surprised and relieved at how quickly the paramedics got Roy onto a stretcher and into the back of the ambulance. Maddy climbed in to ride to the hospital with him so she could tell the medics how they'd found him and what she'd done for him.

Jack yelled, "I'll go call his wife and his son and daughter-in-law." Maddy nodded to show she'd understood and he headed back towards the house, leaning hard into the wind. Then the door was closed and they were on their way. Maddy had never ridden in an ambulance before, and it wasn't nearly as exciting as she had assumed. It was bumpy and she was thrown around and had to hang on to hand holds to keep from falling on Roy and the paramedic. Fortunately, the hospital wasn't far. Nothing was 'far' in Marshallhaven, she thought wryly.

Half an hour later Maddy sunk wearily into the stained and ugly, but relatively comfortable, upholstered waiting room chair. Her clothes were soaked through, but she didn't think another water stain would make that much difference to the chair. Roy was going to be OK. He was responding but wasn't totally conscious yet. He had a bad concussion from that tree branch. Why hadn't he just stopped mowing when the storm started? No one would care if the lawn wasn't perfect. Roy's wife Betty, and their son had already seen him and talked to the doctor. Jack was having a quick prayer with them, and then she could go home.

"You look like a drowned rat," said Jack, standing next to her, "Let me take you home." He helped her to her feet. With the adrenaline rush gone, she was exhausted.

"I'll get you into a hot shower and into bed and then I've got to patch that window before more rain gets in." Maddy just nodded. A hot shower. The thought made her smile.

Sunday morning dawned bright and clear. Maddy burrowed her head into her pillow and groaned. She was still exhausted. Jack was up and showering already. *How come* he *wasn't tired after last night?* she wondered. She dragged herself into a sitting position and just sat there staring at the wall until Jack came back into the bedroom.

"Rise and Shine," he said cheerfully. "How are you feeling?" Maddy just grunted.

"Why don't you just lie down for another half hour?" he said, with concern. "I can make coffee and toast for myself." Maddy flopped sideways back onto the bed. Jack leaned down and kissed her. "Let's see," he said gazing at a row of identical black clerical collars, "What should I wear? Decisions, decisions!" Maddy giggled despite her exhaustion. It was an old joke, but always good for a laugh.

An hour later, Maddy walked over to the church, much refreshed after a shower and a rare-for-her cup of caffeinated coffee. She'd glanced through the paper and came across a short update on the Hendergast case. Someone had found his camper tucked into a grove of trees a little upriver from the park. It apparently hadn't been touched since he'd been murdered and there wasn't much in it besides a few clothes and some rotten food. Not very helpful.

She decided to go over to the church early to help organize the Sunday school children for the Palm Sunday processional, but when she arrived, the only ones there besides Jack and the confirmands were Laura and Babs. Babs was carefully settling the large standing vases with arrangements of palm leaves and long fronds of sweet broom flowers on the steps next to the pulpit and lectern. Her lovely arrangements of passionflower and purple hibiscus were already on the shelves behind the altar.

"No, they won't show up until ten minutes before the start of the service", said Laura with a laugh that contrasted with her sad eyes.

"I should have known," said Maddy. It was typical for the church to be nearly empty at 9:50 and full at 9:59. "I just thought that for Palm Sunday…"

Laura laughed again. "No, no one comes early unless they have a specific reason, like making coffee or setting up communion. They'll be here soon enough, and the Sunday School teachers will be glad of any help in keeping the kids from climbing the walls. How is Roy doing this morning?"

Maddy was surprised, but supposed she shouldn't be. Laura, as usual, knew everything about everyone. "Pastor called the hospital this morning, and he's doing fine. They'll probably keep him another day, but he's alert and eating breakfast. Jack will take him communion this afternoon."

Laura picked up the bulletins and headed for the narthex. Maddy followed and filled her in on how they found Roy unconscious in the storm.

"It's too bad that another window got broken," said Laura as she placed a stack of bulletins at the front and side entrances.

"I know," said Maddy. "I wonder which one was broken last night?" She strolled into the nave and looked for the newly patched window. There it was—The Fall of Jericho. The branch had gone through the lower corner. Right through where the picture of the anvil had been. Maddy's brow wrinkled. Something wasn't right. Two windows broken. Two apparent accidents. Two anomalies likely obliterated. She was assuming that the first one had obliterated an anomaly, but she wasn't completely sure. But this was probably not a coincidence. How could she find out what the first broken window looked like before the baseball went through it? The idea came to her as she looked at the pictures of past confirmation classes in the glass fronted bulletin board in the hallway. Pictures. There had to be pictures of the windows somewhere.

"Laura," she asked as she walked quickly back into the narthex, "Are there any good pictures of the stained-glass windows, you know, before they were broken?"

"Sure. There are some really nice ones in the Church Rebuilding Scrapbook. You know, we took pictures from the groundbreaking to the dedication of the finished building." She walked back to the church office and Maddy followed.

"Can I borrow this for a while?" she asked, taking the large album from the upper shelf that Laura had indicated.

"I think I can find you if you don't bring it back," said Laura, straight-faced.

"It's about Zachariah Hendergast," said Maddy. "I think he put clues into the windows."

"Clues? What kind of clues?" asked Laura.

"Well, pictures. Little pictures that don't belong. Like a hidden picture puzzle. Only I don't know what they mean." She told her what she'd found so far, and her desire to find the murderer so that the weight of suspicion and dread would lift from the town and community. "I keep thinking about motives," she continued, "but none of the people he blackmailed were really hurt, I mean they may have been embarrassed, but no one's lives were ruined or anything."

"Oh, I wouldn't say that," said Laura seriously. "There's Roger McBride for instance."

"Roger? What happened to him?"

"Oh, I forgot you didn't know. Everyone else does, but, well, we don't talk about it. It's kind of complicated. But he blames Zachariah for his divorce. You see, he went to an Ag conference in Chicago, oh, that must have been in the Spring of 1980, before the church burned down. And he spent the night with a prostitute and got one of those STD infections. Well, Zachariah must have found out about it when he was treated with antibiotics, but he must not have done anything about it for some time. It wasn't until a year later when the new church was almost rebuilt that things blew up. He never really specified, but I got the impression that he wasn't about to put up with being blackmailed and Zachariah told his wife. She divorced him and took him to the cleaners. He had to sell the farm and that's when he went to work for the farm machinery store in town. He became so bitter. But old Pastor Schultz worked with him. I'll never forget the day that Roger stood up in front of the congregation and said that he'd sinned and that he knew he was forgiven by God but he wanted the congregation's forgiveness, too. Everyone had been gossiping and talking behind his back, but after that, no one said a thing. Everyone was stunned. But you can't publicly forgive someone and then turn around and gossip about him. Things got better for him, even though he'd lost the farm and his marriage, he did well at the store and spent his time volunteering at the church. It's taken him a long time, but I think he finally let go of the bitterness. I can't imagine what he thought when he heard that Zachariah Hendergast had returned to town and that he had been murdered."

What, indeed, thought Maddy. Now here was a motive for murder. But why would he endorse Hendergast to do the new windows if he was holding this over him? Perhaps he was being blackmailed and the endorsement was his payment to keep quiet. But if that were the case and he fulfilled the terms, why did Hendergast tell Roger's wife anyway? But if Hendergast hadn't yet put the screws to him, maybe he just thought he was best for the job. He could then have felt outraged when Zachariah tried to blackmail him when he'd already done him a good turn.

Something about it didn't quite make sense. One thing was certain, though. Someone had murdered Hendergast, and that someone had probably hit Roy on the head and broken two windows, so it had to be someone connected with the church. But who? Everyone she knew she would swear would never intentionally hurt someone, let alone commit murder. Even Harold Broomfield, as obnoxious as he was, still wouldn't kill anyone. Besides, he seemed to be the only one who really liked Hendergast.

Yet she was finding out things about her neighbors and fellow church members that showed a dark underside to their squeaky-clean exteriors. Roger had gotten an STD from a prostitute; Sarah had had a long-standing affair with Zachariah Hendergast and then been abandoned by him; Lenny's daughter had an illegitimate pregnancy and an abortion. And numerous people had apparently hated Hendergast for his blackmailing. What had they been blackmailed about? Had it been innocent things like Vernella's diverticulitis? Or worse? Things people would kill to keep quiet?

The first kids started arriving and Donald Scott, the Sunday school superintendent, was passing out palm branches.

"Now when the first hymn starts, I'll signal you to start. You'll walk up the center aisle waving your palms and then half will go to the right and half to the left and come back down the side aisles. You'll come back up the center aisle and repeat it until the hymn is finished, and then you'll go sit with your parents. OK? The palms are not toys, they are not baseball bats, and they are not swords!" This last was to two boys who had started fencing with their palms. Maddy moved to separate them and start organizing them into two lines.

It wasn't long before the organ had warmed up with a prelude and began the first hymn. The children marched up the aisle importantly, some waving their palms furiously, others hiding behind them shyly, and all enjoying the attention. They were followed by the crucifer carrying the crucifix on a pole, two acolytes, the five confirmands in their white robes, and finally, Jack in his vestments and red stole. Maddy smiled at him and slipped up the side aisle and into her seat before the children started their way back down. She picked up her hymnal and turned to "All Glory Laud and Honor" and turned to face the cross as it passed. She consciously left space between herself and the end of the pew, to keep her promise to Sarah if she came, but the seat remained empty.

The confirmands stood and faced the congregation. Jack went into the familiar introduction, explaining the public examination and its purpose. The three girls looked confident and even eager to show how well they could answer the questions. The two boys gaped like deer in the headlights. As Jack began asking them questions in turn, Maddy watched as each had his or her own method of answering. The tall blonde girl, Sandy, answered every question immediately and confidently. The next girl, Maria, answered softly in her light Hispanic accent, eyes downcast but flitting up at the end as if looking for affirmation that she had answered correctly. Joshua studied the floor intently before answering, as if he might find the answer spelled out on the carpet. His new, shiny, black shoes looked as stiff and awkward as the rest of him. The short and freckled Tamika grinned and giggled her way through each question that was asked her, and Eddie just looked stunned. Every answer of his started with 'um' and he stumbled painfully over each one. Every time he needed prompting, a red flush climbed from his painfully tight tie to the hairline of his flaming red hair. At last, the final question was asked and answered, and all five sat down looking relieved, even Sandy who sat down primly, demurely crossing her ankles. The congregation also relaxed, having been silently cheering them on and cringing sympathetically with each mistake.

Maddy remembered her own confirmation. She had been confirmed with only one other girl in her class. She remembered the two of them practicing together and answering the questions. How long ago that had been. Yet she still remembered many of the questions and their answers *ver batim*. The confirmands looked so young. Maddy remembered feeling much older than they looked. She sighed. It must be a sign of old age when youth look younger and younger.

The rest of the service was beautiful. She loved the Palm Sunday hymns like "Ride On, Ride On in Majesty" and "Hosanna, Loud Hosanna." They sang the same ones every year, but because those hymns only got sung that one Sunday of the year, they seemed special. After the sermon was the service of confirmation where each of the confirmands promised to keep to the Christian faith, even unto death. After that came the reading of the Passion Narrative and the somber ending to the service, signifying the beginning of Holy Week.

It was over before she knew it and she headed back to the parsonage with the bulky album under her arm. She wanted to start looking at it right away, but she was so tired. A nap would be good. Right after lunch.

Maddy woke from her nap groggy and crabby. The light was almost gone. *What time was it, anyway? Almost five?* She groaned and got up. So much for looking through the album tonight. She just didn't have the energy. And tonight was movie night, too. She looked forward to the Sunday night movie with Jack all week.

Jack was reading the *Advocate* from Thursday in the dining room. "It's aaliiiive!" he intoned in a sepulchral tone, then got up and gave her a kiss. "What are we watching tonight?"

"*Seabiscuit*," answered Maddy.

"The one about the horse?" asked Jack.

"Well, there are several about horses, but yes, it's about a horse," answered Maddy with a laugh. "How is Roy doing?"

She pulled out the popcorn maker and plugged it in. She put some butter in the microwave to melt, and then arranged some crackers, cheese, and cold cuts on a platter with some baby carrots. It would have to do for supper, because she had slept too long to make anything hot.

"He's much better today, but he doesn't remember anything about last night at all. The doctor said that's not uncommon with head wounds." Maddy nodded, remembering this from nursing school. "The last thing he remembers is getting the lawn mower out of the shed and starting the mowing. He doesn't even remember the storm coming in. He has no idea what took him around back of the church where we found him." Jack sighed.

Maddy was frowning. "The window wasn't broken until after he was hit on the head, or at least at the same time. We heard it break. So it must have been something else that attracted his attention." She paused for thought again. "He might even have been knocked out earlier. We don't really know how long he'd been out cold." She explained her thoughts of the morning to Jack—that the window was broken right through the anvil-shaped brick. She trailed off, realizing that none of her conclusions seemed to be particularly surprising to either one of them. They knew there were pictures in the windows, that they meant something to someone and that someone was trying to keep anyone from finding out what it was. And that someone was probably the killer. Well, there was nothing they could do tonight. Jack set up the movie and Maddy moved the snacks to the coffee table.

An hour and a half later, she was snuggled up on the couch with Jack, but she was far from relaxed. Seabiscuit was racing against War Admiral, and they were neck and neck. The popcorn was forgotten as her heart raced with the tension. The jockey had pulled Seabiscuit back, sacrificing an initial lead, as the trainer had instructed. He was giving Seabiscuit a good look at his competition with the idea that he would not want to be beaten by the other horse and would give it his all. Sure enough, Seabiscuit, the smaller, disadvantaged horse, surged ahead of the triple crown winner and won by several lengths. It wasn't just a contest of strength, size, or speed. It was a contest of wills, and Seabiscuit had the stronger will to win.

I'm in a race, thought Maddy suddenly. *A contest of wills with the murderer. Only I don't know what my opponent looks like or where the finish line is.* She reflected that she was racing to decipher the message in the windows before any more got broken and she was racing to identify the killer before anyone else was hurt or killed. Part of her felt that she should be working on the puzzle every waking moment, but she knew that it was an exercise that quickly resulted in brain numbing. But what if someone else was hurt or died before she could figure it out? The scrapbook at first seemed like a hedge against further window breakages, but a quick glance had shown her that the photos diminished the scale to the point that finding anomalies would be difficult. Still, she intended to give it a try tomorrow, with the aid of a magnifying glass. Tomorrow was Jack's day off. He'd probably help, too.

Toward the end of the movie, Maddy began to relax. The movie had a satisfyingly happy ending, and she had become aware of Jack's warm, strong hand around her shoulder. As the movie ended, he moved his hand down to her waist and pulled her closer. She looked up into his clear blue eyes which gazed back with an electric warmth. She sighed. When Jack looked at her like that, her hair became glossier and fuller, her waist was two inches smaller and her legs were two inches longer. The crow's feet around her eyes and the little jowls that had started to appear on her jaw line a few years earlier were gone. She was perfectly proportioned, gorgeous, stunning. Jack leaned over and kissed her slowly and she melted. He used the remote to turn off the television and the DVR, leaving the disc in the player. He stood up and took her hand to lead her toward the bedroom. He stopped to turn out the living room lights, leaned down, nuzzled her ear, and whispered those three special words. "Leave the dishes."

CHAPTER FOURTEEN

Maddy gazed out of the car window as they passed field after field. The dark, freshly turned earth soaked up the sunshine that poured from the clear, blue sky. It didn't matter what fun things they decided to do in Des Moines today, taking a road trip was a nice way to spend Jack's day off. Especially since this week would be so hectic. She could see from horizon to horizon and the sky was breathtaking in its vastness. Although other places they had lived were beautiful, such as the stark mountains of Utah and the lush green hills of the Ozarks, this open country felt like home. Maddy had begun to think that she would feel hemmed in and claustrophobic if they lived anywhere else. She had grown up in Kansas but hadn't felt this connection to the open prairie until they'd moved to Iowa.

Jack had been an Air Force brat and had lived in so many different states and even overseas, that he really didn't have a 'home town' or 'home state'. He'd felt the call to be a pastor when he was sixteen, when his dad was stationed at Little Rock Air Force Base in Arkansas and he'd gone straight to St. Paul's College in Concordia, Missouri after graduating from high school. She started there three years later, and they had met in a creative writing course. The rest, as they say, was history.

The traffic got heavier and civilization more prominent as they approached the suburbs. Soon they were pulling into the parking lot for the Botanical Gardens. Maddy smiled with delight. She'd told Jack to surprise her, and he had. This was one of the things they had always meant to do, but never found the time. It was so nice to walk amongst the lush greenery after the cold, harsh winter. If there was any contradiction between her craving for greenery after an Iowa winter and her earlier thoughts about the grandness of the open prairie, she didn't recognize it. To her, they were two different things. But in addition to leaving behind thoughts of winter, she was also able to leave behind thoughts of the uncertain turn her safe and comfortable life had taken since she'd heard about the murder.

After they were done touring the Gardens, they went downtown to get some lunch.

"I thought we'd walk around downtown a bit," said Jack. He twirled a long strand of linguini around his fork, swiped it through the clam sauce, and conveyed it to his mouth, leaning over his plate to avoid dripping on the napkin in his lap.

Maddy cut her angel hair pasta with the edge of her fork, scooped it up tidily with some tomatoes and capers and chewed contentedly. "Actually, I'd like to visit the two glaziers that bid on the windows in '81."

Jack looked surprised. "Do you think they're still around?"

"Well, they were both in last year's directory," answered Maddy. "That doesn't mean the same people are working there, though. Still, I'd like to try to see if anyone remembers anything." She pushed the last of the chopped tomatoes, olives, and capers onto a piece of garlic bread and carefully bit off the corner.

"As you wish. Where are they located?" asked Jack as he signaled the waiter for the check. He had his credit card out and handed it with the check immediately back to the waiter, a pleasant young man with a pierced eyebrow and a tattoo of a phoenix on the back of his neck.

"One is on east 14th street, and the other is in Ankeny," said Maddy as she pulled out the Google Maps sheets she'd printed out that morning.

"We'll visit the Ankeny one second, as it's on the way home," said Jack. The embellished waiter returned with the credit card receipt and Jack calculated the tip in his head, signed the receipt, and pocketed the yellow copy. Jack got up first and held Maddy's chair for her as she got up.

"Why, thank you kind Sir!" she said. She loved the little courtesies and took Jack's proffered arm with a wide smile.

"This is it, 418 South 14th Street," said Jack as he pulled into the cracked and weed covered parking lot. Maddy looked at her printout and then at the rusted numbers above the boarded-up door. It may have been Don's Glass Art last year, but now it was just an empty building.

"I guess we try the other one, then." She sighed as Jack signaled and pulled out of the parking lot. He turned onto the onramp to interstate 235 and headed north. Within ten minutes they were in the suburb of Ankeny.

"What's the address?" asked Jack, as he exited. Maddy gave him directions at each turn until they arrived at what looked more like a warehouse than a retail business. They parked near the only door that looked like a public entrance.

Jack opened the gunmetal grey door with "American Windows and Floor Coverings" in stock lettering blazoned across it for Maddy and they went in. Surprisingly, there was an attractive reception area with a perky brunette behind the counter. Maddy stepped forward, holding out her hand.

"Hi. I was wondering if there is someone I can talk to who worked here in the early 1980's, around 1981?" The young receptionist smiled and ever so gently took Maddy's fingers in a limp handshake.

"Oh, sure, Gramps was around then. I can go get him, if you'd like." As she spoke, a silver barbell that was stuck through her pierced tongue clacked against her teeth.

The sound made Maddy shiver, like fingernails on a blackboard, but she smiled and said, "Oh, thank you. That would be great!"

The girl bounced through the door behind the counter, making her straightened, shoulder-length hair swish. Maddy raised her eyebrows at Jack but said nothing. Soon a middle-aged man with a serious beer-gut tightly covered with a stained and holey t-shirt came out of the door with the receptionist following. He frowned at Jack and Maddy but extended his hand to Jack.

"I'm Marvin Brown. And you are...?" he said suspiciously.

"I'm Pastor Jack Mitchell at St. Paul Lutheran Church in Marshallhaven. I understand you had submitted a bid to replace the stained-glass windows during the rebuilding of the church in 1981?"

Marvin Brown grunted and said, "You're not the first person to ask about that. I already told that sheriff everything I know, which isn't much. What do you want to know for? I didn't get the bid. Some two-bit 'artiste' got it, and for more than I bid, even."

Maddy asked, "Did they happen to tell you why your bid was rejected? Do you think you would have done a better job?"

"Oh, I don't actually make the windows. I order them from Chicago, and install them. They're custom-made, though, and I do top notch installation work, guaranteed." His chest swelled with pride as he added, "I've never had a dissatisfied customer."

"Did you know anything about the artist who did get the job?" asked Maddy.

"Nope. I'd never heard of him. Had some outlandish name, but I never met him. Like I said, I already told the sheriff all this. I take it that he was killed or something?"

"Can you remember anything else about it?" asked Jack.

"Nope. Just that I missed out on a sweet commission. Of course, as I say, 'Their Loss.'" He said with a smile.

"Of course," said Jack pleasantly. "Sorry to take up your time."

As they walked back toward the car, Jack said gently, "I'm sorry it didn't work out, but I guess I'm not sure what you expected."

"I don't really know either," said Maddy, discouraged. "I should have expected that Joe had already looked them up. There are just so many dead ends. I'm starting to think that it's the perfect murder. Except that the murderer keeps trying to cover things up."

"Like, maybe he'll make a mistake?" asked Jack.

"Yeah, but I'm afraid of what he'll do in the meantime."

On the way home, her underlying uneasiness about the unsolved murder occupied her thoughts. She thought about the scrapbook of the church rebuilding that contained pictures of the windows and resolved to look through it before going to bed.

"What's that?" asked Jack, pointing to one of the pictures.

"It looks like the Good Shepherd window," said Maddy, squinting. The pictures weren't the greatest. Some were polaroids that had faded considerably in the last thirty years. Others were probably taken with a 35 mm SLR and were in somewhat better condition, but the photographer seemed to not understand how to how to construct a scene or focus properly. Many were focused on the faces of the people in the foreground, leaving the detail of the construction in the background hopelessly fuzzy.

The next few pages were of the nearly finished building without people in them and were better focused. At last, three pictures on a page contained close-ups of three of the completed windows, and one of them was the Resurrection window.

"That's it!" whooped Maddy, as she pulled the album closer to try to make out the detail. Jack picked up the magnifying glass he'd dug out of the junk drawer before they started and they bumped heads trying to look through it at the same time.

"I'm sorry, you go ahead," said Jack, laughing and rubbing his head.

Maddy leaned over the picture and peered at it. This was a lot harder than looking at the windows in the church. The photo was so tiny in comparison to the real window; the individual details were downright miniscule.

"I have an idea," said Jack suddenly. He picked up the album and carried into the smallest bedroom that they used as an office. Maddy saw what he was doing and helped position the album on the scanner.

"That's better," he said, once he had scanned the photo at the highest resolution possible. They both sat down and peered at the screen. Jack moved the image slowly from left to right, top to bottom as they examined each section.

"There," said Maddy with certainty. She pointed to the lower right corner.

"By George, I think you've got it," said Jack in a faux British accent. Maddy took out her notebook and began to sketch.

On Tuesday, Maddy quickly ordered her usual and then leaned across the table to Penny. "We found it! The anomaly in the Resurrection window!"

"What!?" she said "What is it?"

"It looks like a fan. You know, an old-fashioned desk fan!" Maddy pulled her little notebook out of her purse and showed Penny a little drawing of it. Penny looked at it and at the graph showing the windows and their corresponding anomalous pictures.

"So where does that leave us? We're still missing two, but the ones we have don't seem to mean anything. You said it's like a hidden object puzzle and we've found most of them, but is that it? Maddy? Hello, Earth to Maddy."

Maddy was gazing off into space. Suddenly her eyes focused on Penny and she said, "It's a rebus."

"You mean like a picture of an olive and a Yule log are read 'I love you'?"

"Yes! That's it exactly." She looked again at her notebook. "Candy canes, something, towels, question mark, fan. Hmmm. It's probably only one word, like 'candy' or 'canes'. And we still need to find the other two."

She frowned and put the notebook back in her purse as her salad and sandwich arrived. She had found that the second window had indeed been broken to obliterate an anomalous picture. That meant it wasn't accidental, and that also meant, as she already had good reason to believe, that Roy's hit on the head wasn't accidental either. She outlined her reasoning to Penny while they ate. It all confirmed her suspicions. It all fit—someone, most likely the murderer, knew about the pictures in the windows and was trying to prevent anyone from deciphering their message.

"Which is all the more reason to figure out what they mean, before more windows get broken, and before someone else gets hurt," said Maddy.

"Show me again what we're missing," said Penny, pushing aside her now empty plate. Maddy reached down for her purse but didn't feel it right away. Thinking she must have kicked it under her chair while she was eating, she backed up and reached further under her chair. When she didn't encounter it, she stood up and started looking around in earnest.

"What's wrong?" asked Penny.

"My purse! It's gone!" said Maddy as a feeling of panic rose up in her. It was definitely not under her chair, under the table, or anywhere nearby. She had just seen it; had put her notebook into it and set it down on the floor less than half an hour ago. She jumped up so fast she knocked her chair over. The noise of it only added to her panic. She looked wildly around the bakery. It had been crowded at lunch time but was now nearly empty. There were two tables close behind where she was sitting, but she had no idea who had been sitting at them.

Suddenly she spotted what looked like her purse, across the room near the exit. She rushed over and picked it up with a sigh of relief, but the relief was short-lived. Her purse had not walked across the room of its own accord. She started emptying the contents onto the table, looking first for the important things: wallet, credit cards, driver's license, cash, house keys, car keys, cell phone—all there. Then the less important things: sunglasses, lipstick, pens, loose change, and the flotsam of miscellaneous items that collect at the bottom. The pile on the table grew until things started to fall off the edge. Penny caught a lipstick rolling toward the edge and picked up a pack of Kleenex and the sunglasses off the floor. It might even be funny if they weren't so intent on the inventory. Everything seemed to be there. Except… except her little notebook.

She looked up at Penny with a pale and frightened face. The train of logic flowed through her mind too quickly to follow, but the conclusion was terrifying. The only person who would steal her notebook but not her credit cards had to be the same person who was trying to break enough windows to prevent anyone from deciphering the windows, and that person was likely the murderer. But now that person was trying to prevent *her*, *Maddy*, from deciphering the windows, and that person had already killed one person and left another unconscious at night in a storm. Roy was elderly. He might have died, would have died, if Jack and Maddy hadn't found him and gotten him to a hospital. How far would the murderer go to prevent her from discovering the truth?

It was all more horribly real than it had been before. There was a murderer in their little community; a murderer who was focused on her—and had been sitting right behind her. Penny was obviously following the same train of thought.

"Promise me you won't go anywhere alone. Even to the church. Or I should say, especially to the church, considering that this person has been lurking around and has vandalized the windows twice, without being seen."

Maddy nodded mutely. She was afraid, but her fear just made her more determined to find the killer. It was the only way to lift the fear. There was a lot going on this week, what with Holy Week services, Easter to plan for, and Mark coming home and bringing his friend with him. But she'd make some time.

"Can you meet me tomorrow after work? We can look at the windows together and try to figure them out."

"Sure," said Penny. She looked as determined as Maddy felt.

There was something else she needed to do in the meantime. On her way home, she stopped at the sheriff's office.

"What can I do for you, Maddy?" Joe asked when he saw her.

"I need to talk to you about the broken window."

"The one broken by the baseball?"

"No. Not the first one, the second one. The one broken in the storm on Saturday night. Well, you know how the first one wasn't an accident? Well, the second one wasn't either." She then outlined her thinking, told him what they'd found in the windows since that first time, and that both windows had been broken right where anomalous pictures had been. "And that means that Roy's accident wasn't accidental, either."

Joe looked thoughtful. "When did you realize that the second broken window wasn't accidental?"

"Well, pretty much by Sunday morning, when I thought through the events of Saturday night. But the implications of it didn't really gel in my mind until just now at lunch, when I was talking it over with Penny."

"So, Roy doesn't know? He still thinks the branch hit him by accident due to the storm?"

"I suppose so. He doesn't remember anything that happened, doesn't even remember going around the back of the church by the window. Should I tell him?"

"No. I think for right now, we should keep this between ourselves. Don't tell anyone except your husband. I've been keeping a closer eye on the church since the first incidence of vandalism, but I have to admit that I didn't think anyone would be out in that storm. I think I'll do more than just drive by from here on out. Maybe walk around the grounds at random times. I'd sure like to catch the culprit." Maddy thought to herself that he certainly would like to catch him, as he was probably more than just a vandal.

"By the way," Joe was saying, "Can you show me what you've found in the windows so far?"

"Actually, I had it all written down in a little spiral notebook, but someone swiped it at lunch today. That was what really convinced me of the connection between the broken windows and the murder." She told him about her purse being taken and left intact except for the notebook. Joe looked at her sharply, then quickly rearranged his face into mild skepticism.

Looking down at his desk, he asked, "So you think the vandal is definitely the murderer?" Maddy nodded. Joe looked thoughtful. "I might agree with you. I'm not sure yet. But if that's true, you could be in danger. I know I can't tell you to stop trying to figure out this little puzzle, and it's probably too late now anyway. You realize that if the murderer is the vandal, he now knows that you're close to figuring this thing out, and whatever it means, he's been trying to prevent it getting out." Maddy nodded again. "Be careful. This isn't just an intellectual exercise. Whoever is behind this has murdered one person and put another in the hospital."

Maddy nodded again. "I know. It really just hit me today. I promised Penny I wouldn't go anywhere alone, wouldn't go over to the church alone."

"Good. I don't suppose you tried to find out who was sitting near your table and could have taken your purse?" Joe asked skeptically.

"Umm. Yes. Well, we tried. Sarah and Donna remembered plenty of the lunch customers, but unfortunately, they couldn't remember who sat where."

"Who did they remember being there at lunch?"

"Oh, all the regulars— Roger McBride, Stan Johnson, and Lenny Carlisle, Darlene Nordquist and her mother, Laura and Ronald, Marlene and Doris, Cindy Oswald and her three kids, the Noon Kiwanis club in the side room…" Maddy went on listing a good number of people.

"I get the picture. No strangers? No suspicious behavior?" Maddy shook her head. Joe sighed.

"Are you any closer to finding the killer?" Maddy asked.

Joe looked askance at her. Was she suggesting that he wasn't doing his job? "No, not really," he said finally. "Like I said before, no one admits to knowing he was back in town. We searched his camper and came up with zilch. No cell phone, no notes with names or phone numbers, not even a checking account to see if he had any influx of funds or what businesses he might have frequented. As far as we can tell, he lived a very simple life with no bank account, no credit cards, no phone. I suppose it's in keeping with his hippie values, but it sure doesn't help us any. I've been trying to find out where he's been for the past thirty years, but it's slow going. We know where he was about ten to fifteen years ago, but we can't find out where he's been recently. Usually, we can track people by credit card or check purchases, or phone calls, but like I said, he didn't use any of those. It would have been so nice if he'd had a note clutched in his hand that read 'meet me in the park' and signed by the murderer. I'd be happy with just the murderer's initials. But I guess that sort of thing only happens in the movies."

"Well, I'll keep praying for you," said Maddy. Joe relaxed and smiled as he saw her to the door.

"One last thing," Joe asked, "Do me a favor, and let me know if you figure anything else out with your window puzzle, would you?"

On the way home, Maddy drove down Main street looking at the river levels. It definitely looked higher. She parked near the Dollar Store and walked around back to look at the sandbag wall. This bank was higher than a few blocks down where they had built the wall, and she had a good view due to the bend in the river. The water level was definitely higher. It was lapping gently against the sandbags, from the looks of it about three feet from the top. Farther out in the river, the current surged, moving remarkably fast. So much water, so much pressure. Pressure. That was what she was feeling. Pressure to solve the puzzle, pressure to find the murderer, pressure to prevent further harm to others or herself. Usually watching the river was relaxing, but not today. Maddy stood up suddenly and walked back toward her car.

Chapter Fifteen

All day Wednesday, Maddy tried to put thoughts of the murder out of her mind. Jack had been as concerned as Penny when she filled him in Tuesday night. He reiterated the instruction to not go anywhere alone as he headed off to the church office that morning. She thought that if he and Laura were at the church, it should be pretty safe, but the seriousness of the situation had been impressed on her by Joe's concern, so she didn't argue. She couldn't do anything until later anyway, and besides, she had a lot of work to do.

She started by mixing up a loaf of cracked wheat bread with sesame and flax seeds, kneading it and setting it to rise. She used to knead her bread by hand, but now she had a beautiful Kitchenaid Professional Series mixer with a dough hook that did the work for her. She'd wanted one for some time but had felt that the expense was too much for the household budget. Two years ago, when Mark was a junior in high school, he and Joanna had gone to Des Moines on Black Friday to do some Christmas shopping at the early morning sales. Joanna had relayed to her later how the two of them were walking through Dillards looking at the displays when they walked by a mountain of Kitchenaid mixers. Mark had stopped so suddenly that Joanna had run into the back of him and nearly fallen over.

"Mom wants one of those!" he had announced to the world at large, pointing dramatically. Seeing that it was fabulously discounted, they'd grabbed a white one off the top, headed for the checkout, and proudly carted their booty to the car.

It was only when they got there that they realized that it wouldn't fit anywhere in Mark's tiny, two-door Civic but in the front passenger seat. It also brought to mind the problem of keeping it secret until Christmas. Maddy still had no idea how they'd gotten it into the house and where they'd stashed it. The monstrous box had mysteriously shown up under the Christmas tree on Christmas Eve, fully wrapped in blue snowflake wrapping paper and topped with a huge silver bow. The two of them had squirmed like kindergarteners while she opened it, hardly able to stand the wait to see her face when she realized what it was. She herself had squealed like a girl when she got the miles of wrapping paper off of it and had to be restrained from opening the box and setting it up right then and there.

Maddy smiled with the memory as she washed the six-quart mixing bowl, dried it and placed it back on the machine.

She cleaned the house from top to bottom and put fresh sheets on the twin beds in Mark's room. She planned out menus, focusing on foods that were fairly familiar, commonly liked, and easy to make ahead, like lasagna and tuna casserole. For Easter dinner, she thought she'd try to find some lamb chops. But if not lamb, then the traditional ham. Let's see, what to go on the side. Rice or potatoes? Wild rice pilaf would go very well with lamb. And, of course, side veggies and dessert. Hmmm. Pie would be good. Lemon meringue. Or Key Lime? No, definitely lemon meringue. She nodded to herself, satisfied with the holiday menu, and made out a shopping list.

By then it was time to deflate the dough and form the loaf. She tipped the dough out onto her oiled countertop, flattened it, folded it, and then formed it into a round loaf. She laid a piece of plastic wrap lightly over the top to keep it from drying out during the final rise and checked her watch. If she was efficient, she could run to the IGA and finish her shopping within the hour and a half rising time.

She considered shopping to not be "alone" because there were people around, yet she still had the constant urge to look over her shoulder. Many of the faces she encountered in the parking lot and store were familiar, but as she reflected on what she had learned about people she thought she knew, she wondered what was behind those familiar innocent faces. Could one of them be the murderer?

"Paper or plastic?" The bored voice of Darlene Nordquist, at the checkout, broke through her reverie.

"Hmmm? Oh, sorry, plastic please." She focused on writing out her check and smiled at Darlene.

"Is everything OK? You look kind of… I don't know… worried," Darlene asked.

"No, no, just, you know, holiday preparations and everything, Easter. And Holy Week. And…" She let her voice trail away, aware that she was starting to babble. She smiled reassuringly at Darlene and wheeled her cart towards the door. "Have a blessed Easter!" she said cheerily in parting.

She made it home with a half hour to spare. She put the baking stone in the oven with a cast iron skillet on the lower shelf and preheated it to 425 degrees. Then she put away the groceries and focused on her housework.

Twenty minutes later she uncovered her loaf, slashed an 'X' in the top, slid it carefully onto the hot baking stone, and poured a half cup of boiling water into the hot skillet to make steam. She checked it every ten to fifteen minutes until it was golden brown and crusty. It sat cooling on the rack when, finally, four o'clock arrived, as did Penny.

The first thing Maddy did was pull out the new little spiral notebook she'd picked up at the IGA and started re-creating the chart of the windows. It wasn't too difficult, and she wondered briefly what the thief thought to accomplish.

"You're thinking about it the wrong way round," said Penny. "This won't keep you from knowing what you already know, but it will tell *him* how much you know and how close you are to solving it."

"Mmm, yes, you're right," said Maddy. "Which means we have to solve it now as soon as we can!" They went over to the church together, stopping in to say hello to Jack on their way to the nave, and started studying the last two windows. Maddy was examining the Temptation of Adam and Eve section by section when she heard Penny exclaim.

"Come here! I think I found something!" She crossed to the other side of the church to look at the Baptism of Jesus. "Here, in this little swirl of water. I think it's a butterfly." Maddy looked closely.

"Yep, I think that's it. But it's not a butterfly. It's a moth."

Penny looked at her incredulously. "How can you tell that?"

"Because it has fuzzy antennae. Look!"

Penny looked again and gaped. "That's incredible detail!"

"I know," said Maddy. "The more I study these windows, the more amazed I am by Hendergast's talent." She sighed. What a waste. He would no longer create such beautiful glasswork. On the other hand, he would no longer create twisted monstrosities either, or blackmail anyone else for that matter. Still, he hadn't deserved to be murdered.

They went back to the last window, but by the time Jack was ready to head home, they still hadn't found anything. All three went back to the parsonage and had a light supper of black beans and rice with fresh bread and steamed carrots, and then Maddy and Penny sat at the table scrutinizing the chart while Jack went into the office to check e-mail.

"Let's see. You said the towels looked like 'his and hers'." Maddy wrote 'His and Hers' in the box, next to 'Towels'.

"The first one is either 'candy' or 'canes'. 'Candy' seems most likely, with 'Can' being the first word in the solution and the 'dee' sound being the first part of the next word. Only 'deemoth' isn't a word."

"What about the question mark?"

"It could be 'mark' or it could be like a sound or word represented by the question mark. You know, like 'huh?' or 'what?'"

Maddy looked thoughtful for a minute and then said, "The five question words are 'who, what, why, where, and when'. I suppose it could be any one of them." She made notes on the chart.

"What about the horse?" said Penny musingly.

"I suppose it could be 'horse, stallion, mare, colt, filly, or gelding'." Maddy made some more notes.

"Let me try out some combinations and see how they sound," said Penny. She began reading the first five in different combinations. "Candy moth towels mark fan. Candy moth his mark fan. Candy moth hisandhers what fan." Maddy shook her head each time. Nothing made sense. When they'd been at it for over an hour, reading different word combinations with different inflections, Maddy felt like her brains were being scrambled. "I don't think we're getting anywhere," she said.

"Me neither," said Penny. "When the dining room table starts to look like a comfortable place to lie down and sleep, it's definitely time to go home. When shall we get together to try this again?"

"With you working and Maundy Thursday and Good Friday services, it will have to be Saturday morning," answered Maddy.

"OK. See you then!" Penny picked up her purse and headed to the door. She turned back as a thought occurred to her. "Mark will be home, won't he? Are you sure you want to spend time on this instead of with him?"

"Oh, we won't spend all day at it. Besides, he's bringing a friend and they'll probably want to do some things together. They'll probably want to sleep in on Saturday, too." She smiled. "It'll be fine."

Maddy walked wearily into the computer room where Jack was just getting up from the desk chair. He gave Maddy a quick kiss and moved over to the saggy old love seat that occupied the corner. Maddy sat down in front of the computer and Allegro immediately jumped into her lap and started purring and kneading her thigh. Maddy petted her contentedly while she navigated to her webmail site. It had been a long morning, baking bread and preparing the house for the weekend. She saw with pleasure that there were three e-mails from the kids in her inbox. She opened the first one.

To: channelingkatie@cable.com

From: theonlyolnies@nbx.com

Subject: You're going to be a grandmother soon!

Mom,

I just got back from my OB-Gyn and he said that this baby could come any time! I am *so* ready. My ankles are so swollen that I can't wear any of my shoes anymore except the sneakers with all the laces taken out. I don't feel bad, really, just like a beached whale whenever I try to move. And hungry all the time! I'll keep you posted.

Love,

Martha

Maddy excitedly relayed the information to Jack, thinking of holding her first grandchild. How nice to cuddle and play with a baby, and then hand him back to Martha when his diaper was full. She moved on to the next one.

To: channelingkatie@cable.com

From: adaspira@mit.edu

Subject: Re: Re: Easter

Mom,

Thanks for being so understanding. I really will miss being home for Easter, but it's not like I'll be alone. Seamus and I are going to the Easter sunrise service at St. Paul's Cathedral. It's such a beautiful church, I'm sure the service will be gorgeous! Then he's taking me to brunch at Changsho Restaurant. I can't wait! I've also talked to Seamus about coming to visit you and Dad. I just know you'll love him! He's just wonderful. He said he doesn't want to get in the way of my spirituality and would never keep me from going to church. Isn't that great? And I just know I can get him to come with me eventually.

I can't wait to see my new niece or nephew! Any word yet on when he or she is coming?

BTW, I've started a new Facebook page. You should sign on, too. That way we can share pictures and stuff more easily. You might be able to connect with some old friends, too. I've found some high school friends that I'd lost touch with. It's free and it's easy. Mark has a Facebook page, too. You could keep up with what he's doing while he's at school. Just a thought.

Talk to you later,

Love,

Joanna

Maddy forwarded Martha's e-mail to both Joanna and Mark so they'd know the latest news. She'd have to think about the Facebook thing. She really didn't think anyone was interested in what she had for breakfast or any other random thoughts that seemed to be the stuff of most posts, nor did she have the patience to sit down every day and post.

She turned to Jack. "Did you know that Joanna has a new boyfriend?"

Jack looked up from his book. "What? No. Who is he?"

Maddy pursed her lips. "I forgot to tell you. Joanna called last week. She's definitely head over heels, but I'm not sure what to think of him. His name is Seamus. She described him as 'an artist'. What really bothered me is that she also described him as an unchurched spiritualist. I think she said something like 'he believes in God but doesn't feel the need to go the church' when I asked if he was a Christian. And just now, in her e-mail, she pretty much indicated that he's 'letting' her go to church on her own but has no intention of attending himself. He is going to be going to church with her on Easter, but they're going to a Catholic cathedral instead of a Lutheran church. Like it's more of a show than worship. I don't know. I just don't feel good about it."

Jack raised an eyebrow. "And what are you going to do about it?"

"Well, she's an adult. There's not much I can do, except try to get to know who he really is and be there for Joanna. I guess that's really what has me worried. I think he's going to hurt her. You know, emotionally. If she is emotionally involved with someone who doesn't share her faith, it will eventually hurt her, whether he means to or not."

Jack looked thoughtful, and then nodded. "I agree. I think we should meet this Seamus. Have you invited him to visit?"

"Of course! It was the first thing I did!" She sighed. "And maybe we'll meet him and find out that he intends to start going to church after all, and is a really wonderful person and good to Joanna. It's what I'd like to believe anyway. She said maybe they'd visit around the end of May."

"Well, that's not too far off, then. And we'll get to know Seamus." Jack smiled reassuringly and went back to reading.

Allegro, finally tired of kneading, jumped down, trotted over to Jack, and curled up in his lap, her light calico fur contrasting with his black clerical collar.

Maddy turned her attention to the e-mail from Mark.

To: channelingkatie@cable.com

From: themathguy@ui.edu

Subject: Good Friday

Hi, Mom!

The car's all packed and ready so Kim and I can leave after our last class, which ends around 11. Then it's Iowa City in the rear view mirror—at least for the weekend. J

Love ya,

Mark

Maddy was curious to meet Kim. With a name like that she wondered if he was Asian, too. Kim was a common Korean men's name. It wouldn't surprise her if Mark had made friends with other Asian kids. Growing up in rural Iowa meant that he was usually the only non-white kid in his class. He had graduated with a few Hispanic kids, but no African-Americans or other Asians. He'd been teased at first, but he quickly turned into the class clown and was able to deflect the teasing. As the other kids got to know him, he made friends and the teasing dropped off. Still, he was experiencing a much more diverse community at college and was bound to gravitate towards people who shared a common heritage and a common appearance.

Maddy played a couple games of Solitaire on the computer until she realized how late it was.

Thursday was another busy day. She planned to prepare a tuna casserole and a white lasagna with sausage and spinach for Friday's and Saturday's dinners respectively, and the wild rice pilaf for Sunday. She had the casserole and the pilaf finished by the time Jack showed up. Lunch needed to be quick, with Jack needing to prepare a little more for tonight's Maundy Thursday service. It would also be First Communion for the five 8th graders who had been confirmed on Sunday. Maddy had sandwiches already made and poured milk for the two of them.

Jack perused the morning's *Advocate* while he ate. "Looks like the river's crested," he said between bites.

"And not a moment too soon. Any higher and the sandbags might have failed. It'll take some time to go down, though." He folded up the paper, gulped the last of his milk, and got up. "Sorry to eat and run," he grinned. Maddy smiled as he walked briskly back to the church, then pulled out the recipe for lasagna.

When she had first started cooking from scratch, back when she'd stopped working full time, she had been surprised at how much time it took on the one hand, yet if she planned ahead and deliberately made extra or make-ahead dishes, she could save time. So, making three full dishes today took the entire morning and most of the afternoon, but she wouldn't need to do any more real cooking until Sunday. Except the pie, she reminded herself. She'd need to make that on Saturday.

The lasagna finally in the oven, she sat down to read the newspaper. RIVER CRESTS TWO FEET ABOVE FLOOD STAGE read the headline. It continued:

"The Army Corps of Engineers confirmed that the river has crested, and levels have dropped one half inch in the last twelve hours. At two feet above the moderate flood stage, the river threatened to flood downtown Marshallhaven, but the dedication of the volunteers who built the sandbag wall has saved several businesses from damage. Water levels are expected to recede steadily barring any further rainfall. No rain is forecast for the next three days, and then only a thirty percent chance on Monday. "It looks like we dodged the bullet this year," said Mayor Horace Weatherby. "Thanks to our volunteers who have not only spared our town, but shown us what it means to be a part of a community. Once the water recedes, volunteers will again be needed to remove the sandbags, but that won't be for several weeks." The Corps of Engineers projects a recession rate of two to five inches per week based on the current speeds and the level of snowpack remaining upriver."

Maddy put the paper down. Well, there was one thing less to worry about. She still felt the weight of having a murderer at large, the stress of Holy Week, and the anxiety about Joanna's new boyfriend, but she was thankful that the town would not suffer flood damage.

Supper, like lunch, was a hurried affair. Jack headed straight back over to the church after finishing his chili. Maddy quickly followed after rinsing and stacking the dirty dishes in the sink, grabbing her purse, and pulling the locked door closed behind her. Once there, she seated herself and collected her thoughts. Maundy Thursday, the commemoration of Jesus' institution of the Lord's Supper. Such a fitting time for the eighth graders' First Communion, she thought. She focused on the comfortingly familiar service right through to the end, when the altar and pulpit were stripped of their paraments in preparation for the starkness of Good Friday. After the Maundy Thursday and Good Friday services, everyone was expected to leave the church in silence, contemplating the events of Holy Week. Maddy left, knowing Jack would be along soon.

She crossed the dark parking lot alone, the other worshippers leaving as quietly and quickly as she, without the usual chatting and well wishes. It had become dark during the service, and as she came abreast of the single street light, it went out. She sighed in exasperation. Why did street lights do that? It was as if they had some kind of motion sensor and went dark just when extra light would be most welcome. Shouldn't it work the other way around? She'd forgotten to leave the front porch light on, too, because it had still been light when they'd left, and she was in such a hurry. Now she would have to fumble in her purse for her keys.

She undid the flap and started reaching around, pushing aside her wallet and cell phone, to try to feel around the bottom. Hmmm. Her hand touched something sticky—an old cough drop that had come unwrapped and absorbed the moisture from the air until it was soft and tacky. Ugh. She wiped her hand ineffectually on a Kleenex and tried to peer into the depths. There was no moon to help out either. She sat on the front porch and turned so as to take advantage of the dim and distant light from the garage lights two doors down, such as it was. She pulled out her wallet, cell phone, and checkbook, set them on the step, and recommenced her search. Still nothing. She shook the purse gently to listen for the jingle of keys, but the motion elicited nothing but a dull rustle. She sat for a moment, thinking. When had she last used her keys? Yesterday? It must have been yesterday when she went shopping. She closed her eyes and pictured coming home from the store. She'd set her purse and keys on the dining room table and then put away the groceries. Then when she'd cleared the table for supper, she'd moved both purse and keys to the top of the entertainment center. Jack must have moved her purse sometime later to their bedroom, but probably hadn't seen the keys next to it. Why had she locked the door? It was all due to this murder business, upsetting her regular routines. OK, all the activity of Holy Week was also adding stress, but usually that was a good kind of stress. A holiday kind of stress. But the murder had brought up so much ugliness and uncertainty.

Maddy looked across the now empty parking lot, hoping to see Jack coming home, but the parking lot was still empty. She started to shiver. It was getting cold fast. *Better to be moving than to be sitting still*, she thought, and started walking back to the church.

She headed around the corner towards the door to Jack's study, and was surprised at how much darker it was on this side. There had at least been a little ambient light from houses and farther street lights on the parking lot side of the church, but here was nothing but trees and the darkened building.

Suddenly she stopped and spun around. She'd seen something move—in the darkness between the trees. Or she thought she had seen something out of the corner of her eye, but now everything was still. She could smell the wild nighttime odors of trees and grass and the dusty smell peculiar to parking lots. No wind. No clouds. No moon. Just clear black sky with hundreds of stars. It would have been a breathlessly beautiful sight, if it hadn't been so cold and getting colder by the minute. And if she wasn't so jittery from the adrenaline racing through her veins from the imagined movement. She calmed her ragged breathing and turned back toward the church.

She whipped around, certain that this time she had definitely heard something. Her heart raced as she staggered, turning her head this way and that, feeling both frightened and foolish. Was there a shadow moving in the trees? She called out, "Who's there?" but her voice was a high-pitched raspy squeak.

Something moved again and started moving towards her. It was so dark, she could only make out a roughly human form. A huge human form. She turned and ran. Or tried to run. She stumbled toward the church door, so near, yet so far. Jack was close—just the other side of that door. If she could just reach it.

Without warning she was down on the ground. She'd tripped on something, twisting her ankle in the bargain. Pain shot through her ankle as she twisted around. She knew she couldn't stand, let alone run. She turned to see the figure advancing on her, a hand raised. She tried to scream, but her throat felt like construction paper. "Help!" came from her mouth, a pathetic mewling. She swallowed, trying to moisten her mouth, but no saliva came. *I'm going to die*, she thought in a cold, detached part of her mind. *I'm going to be murdered, on Maundy Thursday, outside the church, just a few feet away from Jack on the other side of the wall.* If only she'd solved the puzzle faster. If only she'd remembered her keys. If only she'd called Jack with her cell phone before heading back to the church. Her head was filled with 'if onlys' that didn't matter at all now. The figure was upon her, and she flinched in anticipation of the blow.

Something seemed familiar about the way the figure moved. The profile of a man was outlined against the stars. And the raised hand was reaching down to grasp her arm.

"Are you all right, Madalyn?" came a familiar voice, and strong gentle hands were helping her up. She looked into the face of Stan Johnson. Stan! It was only Stan. In the rush of relief, she felt ridiculous as well.

"Stan! It's you! I mean, I couldn't tell who it was." She laughed, noting the note of hysteria in her voice. "I... I... um, I saw something move and I thought..." She stopped and winced as she tried to stand on her ankle.

"Maddy? Is that you?" The warm yellow light from the study spilled out into the dark and Jack was running towards the two of them. Maddy fell into his arms and realized that she was shaking.

She laughed again, this time trying to act and sound normal. "I forgot my keys and was coming back, when I saw something moving in the trees and I thought... well, I thought of Roy and well... so silly of me really. It was only Stan. And I tripped and twisted my ankle."

Jack looked questioningly at Stan, who cleared his throat.

"I'm so sorry to have scared you like that. I should have said something. I guess I didn't realize you couldn't see me or see who I was." He turned to Jack and continued. "I was checking the shed. Didn't want the lawnmower to get left out again. Then I saw Madalyn alone in the dark, and I came to see if she was OK, and she fell."

"Well, I'm glad you were here," said Jack. "I was taking longer than I expected, finalizing some last-minute changes to tomorrow's sermon. These walls are so thick, I wouldn't have heard her if she'd fallen and you weren't here to help her. Thanks." He extended his hand and Stan shook it.

"Well, I should be going home," Stan said with a small smile. "Janet and Lawrence will be wondering where I've gotten to. She drove separately and should already be home by now. You should get some ice on that ankle," he finished, looking at Maddy. She nodded mutely. He looked back at Jack as if he'd had a new thought. "Has Harold Broomfield been talking to you?" he asked.

Jack nodded. "Why? What have you been hearing?"

Maddy shivered as she clung to Jack and her teeth were chattering, more from the fright and the rush of relief than from cold.

"You must be freezing!" said Jack sympathetically. "Come on. Let's get you inside." He kissed her forehead and led her into his study, Stan following.

She sat down in the easy chair and massaged her ankle while Stan sat in the hard chair across from Jack. What an idiot she'd been, running and screaming like a pre-teen at a campfire ghost story fest. Not only had she embarrassed herself in front of Stan, she now had a sore ankle to boot.

"Harold's been talking to some of the elders," Stan was saying. His face was a combination of irritation and amusement. "He's trying to get them stirred up with this 'some people don't like the pastor' nonsense." He snorted. "We all know he using the journalistic 'some'. You know—'some people think' and 'some people say' which really means 'I think'".

"So, you really don't think there are any others?" Jack asked carefully.

"No. I tried to get him to cough up a name, but he just got vaguer and waffled around saying things like they didn't want to be identified and were too intimidated to talk to anyone else, etcetera, etcetera. And the number of people who are supposedly upset is like the fish that got away. It gets bigger with every telling." Stan grinned a toothy grin and then his face became serious again. "I'd had enough, so I leaned on Harold pretty hard. I told him I knew for a fact that it was a bunch of nonsense and implied that if he continued this disrespectful treatment of the pastor, gossip, and outright lies that the elders might have to use the Matthew 18 process to 'exhort him to repent of his sins'".

Maddy was impressed. Stan had subtly, or not so subtly, threatened Harold with excommunication. Church discipline was hardly ever exercised anymore. It was unlikely that someone in Harold's position would really be brought before the congregation or that he would actually be excommunicated. But the threat had probably let Harold know that he wasn't going to find any support amongst the church leadership and that he would be watched.

Jack raised an eyebrow, his expression echoing some of Maddy's thoughts.

Stan continued confidently. "The other two elders present, although mostly silent and a little sheepish, were clearly in agreement with me and Harold actually looked nervous. I don't think you'll be hearing any more of his nonsense. And if you do, I want to hear about it." Stan stood to take his leave.

"Sure thing. And... thanks." Jack stood up and gripped Stan's proffered hand. Stan nodded politely at Maddy and closed the study door behind him.

Maddy stood up and tested her ankle. It was already feeling better. Not a bad sprain, then, just a minor twist. Thank God for small favors.

They walked home, Maddy leaning on Jack's arm, and Jack used his keys to get into the house.

"I thought your keys were in your purse," he said, when she explained again about forgetting her keys. "I moved your purse, but I thought your keys were in it. I'm so sorry."

"It's not your fault," said Maddy. She retrieved her keys from the top of the entertainment center and put them back in her purse. She stared at her purse for a minute lost in thought.

"Is something wrong?" asked Jack.

"Hmmm? No. It's just that something doesn't seem right, but I can't put my finger on it. Oh, well. It'll come to me." She walked to the kitchen and got some ice out of the freezer. She wasn't even limping anymore, but the ice couldn't hurt. She took two

Advil, sat down on the couch with her Sudoku book, and put the plastic bag of ice on her ankle.

"You go to bed, Jack. You need the sleep. I'll be in soon." Jack smiled and kissed her before going down the hall to the bathroom.

CHAPTER SIXTEEN

"Oh, my goodness, is it two already?" Maddy gasped as Mark's little blue Civic pulled into the driveway. The morning had rushed by as she made last minute preparations. Her ankle was mostly pain free if she didn't turn it too much. She'd managed to get everything done that she'd wanted except some of the laundry. Oh, well. It could wait until next week. At least there were plenty of clean towels.

She resisted the urge to crane her neck at the window to try to catch a glimpse of Kim, but instead set out some veggies and dip in case they were hungry. Young men were always hungry, in her experience. The door opened and she turned to see Mark sticking his head in.

"Hi, Mom! We're here!" Then he stepped aside, and just as Mark was saying, "Mom, I'd like you to meet Kimberly", a lithe, pretty African American girl with intelligent and laughing eyes stepped through the door.

Maddy's jaw dropped. She quickly adjusted her face into a welcoming smile, said "Kimberly, it's so nice to meet you!" and gave her a quick hug. "Come in, make yourself at home. There're some snacks on the table if you're hungry, and if you'll excuse me, I'll get your room ready." She gave Mark a pointed look and went to make up Joanna's room for her.

As she turned the corner and opened the linen closet, she heard Kimberly say in a low voice, "She looked kind of shocked when you introduced me. Is it because I'm black?"

Mark laughed. "Nnnooo. I think it's because you're female."

"What!? You didn't tell her I was coming?"

"Well, sure, I told her I was bringing a friend, but now that I think about it, I kind of forgot to tell her you were my *girl*friend." She heard what sounded like a punch and heard Mark say "Oww! One measly little detail! Besides, you couldn't really think my parents are prejudiced! I mean... look at me!" thump "Oww! Stop it!" But soon it sounded like she was doing something else, something he didn't want her to stop.

Maddy grinned and continued down the hall with the clean sheets. It occurred to her that the latest arrival from Netflix, although apropos, was probably not the best choice for the weekend's entertainment. It was the movie *Guess Who?*, a modern comedic remake of the old black and white *Guess Who's Coming to Dinner?*. Like the various sets of parents in the two movies, she was definitely surprised, but unlike the fictional families, she was delighted. Mark hadn't dated much in high school, beyond asking a girl to the prom, and she'd sometimes wondered if he'd feel more comfortable with a non-white girlfriend.

"So, Kimberly, tell me about yourself," said Jack in between bites of lasagna. He was trying to be sociable and eat quickly at the same time. Good Friday service would be starting in an hour and a half.

"Well, I'm from the Quad Cities—Bettendorf—I'm a freshman, and I'm majoring in music education and organ." Kimberly took a piece of garlic bread and passed the plate to Mark. He took the plate from her, deliberately brushing her fingers in the process.

"That's interesting," said Maddy. "Have you thought about being a church organist?"

"Yes. I can already play hymns on the piano, and I know what a shortage there is of organists. I've always loved the pipe organ, but I also play the trumpet, the clarinet, and the soprano saxophone."

"So what church were you raised in?" asked Jack.

"Well, my Mom is Lutheran and my Dad is Presbyterian. We kind of went to both while I was growing up. My sisters and I used to call ourselves 'Lutheterians'. But I've been going to church with Mark, and I really like it." She smiled at Mark who smiled soppily back. *Yep*, Maddy thought, *he's got it bad. And she seems like such a nice girl. First Joanna, and now Mark. It must be Spring. 'Love is in the air' and all that.* She smiled at her thoughts and passed Mark another serving of lasagna.

Maddy then asked Mark about his classes and extracurricular activities so Kimberly wouldn't feel like she was getting the third degree. It was a topic that Kimberly could feel included in and she joined in the conversation about college life.

"Maddy and I met at college," Jack commented with a smile. "I was a senior when she was a freshman. One more year and I would have missed her!" he said in mock distress. They all laughed, and Maddy noted how easily Kimberly fit into the family circle.

After Jack had excused himself and went back to the church, and Mark had finished his third serving of lasagna, Maddy started cleaning up. Kimberly immediately jumped up and offered to help.

"Thank you!" said Maddy, "So, have you ever been to a Good Friday Tenebrae service?" she asked while rinsing and loading the dishes into the dishwasher.

"No, but Mark described it. It's a service of darkness, right?"

"That's right. As the readings progress through the passion narrative, ending with the crucifixion and burial, the church lights are slowly darkened until it's completely black. The only light left is the Christ candle which is briefly removed to symbolize Christ being dead and in the tomb, but it's brought back in and left in the sanctuary to remind us that Jesus will rise again. We'll all leave in silence, and there's no benediction, just like last night, because the three services, Maundy Thursday, Good Friday, and Easter

Vigil are really one interrupted service, called the Holy Triduum—The Holy Three Days. We'll have Easter Vigil tomorrow night, and the scripture readings go through the whole Bible, telling the story of our creation, fall into sin and our salvation. It's a longer service, but we don't pull an all-nighter like they did in the mediaeval church. It used to be all night, flowing right into Easter Sunrise service."

Kimberly laughed. "Um, yeah, I'm glad we're not staying up all night. But it sounds interesting. We never had Easter Vigil at either the Lutheran or Presbyterian churches when I was growing up."

"I'm not surprised," said Maddy, "There are still a lot of Lutheran churches that don't hold Easter Vigil. But it's a beautiful tradition that is experiencing a bit of a comeback."

"By the way, do you prefer to be called 'Kim' or 'Kimberly'?"

"Either one is fine," said Kimberly with a smile. "I was always 'Kimberly' growing up, but my school friends always seemed to shorten it to 'Kim'. As long as you don't call me 'Kimmie'!" She made a 'yuk' face.

"Were you teased by that name?"

"Not really. It's just that my grandmother insisted on calling me 'Kimmie' and my sister 'Ricky' in her sickly-sweet voice. We hated it. My sister's name is Erica," she added by way of explanation.

Maddy nodded, then asked a little sheepishly, "What's your last name? I just realized I didn't know it."

"Didn't Mark tell you anything about me?" asked Kimberly, looking a little aghast.

"Um. No." said Maddy wryly. "He just said he was bringing a friend, Kim."

"That explains your look of astonishment when we met." Kimberly's eyes were laughing, and the corners of her mouth twitched.

Maddy just smiled and turned toward the back of the house where Mark had been seen taking their luggage. "Mark!" she called, "Let's go!"

After the service, the two couples walked back in silence across the parking lot; Jack and Maddy, Mark and Kimberly, both couples holding hands. Kimberly had absorbed the service with wide eyes as the church got darker and darker. She had jumped at the *Strepitus*—the loud sound produced by the closing of a large book when the Christ candle was removed from the sanctuary, symbolizing the closing of the tomb and evoking the despair felt by the disciples. She, Maddy, had jumped, too, and she had been expecting it. This was such a somber time, reflecting on our sin, and the price Jesus paid to redeem us from it. It occurred to her that the price, Jesus' suffering and death, paid for all sins, even the ones that had so shocked her lately—assault, vandalism, lying, blackmail, adultery, and even murder. Free forgiveness was available to any who repented and believed the promise. But *was* there repentance and faith? In Zachariah Hendergast *or* his murderer? She had no idea, but she'd leave that to God.

"Thanks for coming so early," said Maddy to Penny in hushed tones as she opened the door the next morning. "Mark and Kimberly are still asleep. At least their doors are both closed," she added as explanation for her whispering.

"Kimberly?" Penny asked with raised eyebrows. Maddy explained. "Well, that's nice. Do you think it's serious?"

"Only time will tell," said Maddy. "Of course, they're madly in love now, but we'll have to wait until the infatuation wears off a little to see if it will last."

"Well, we'll be quiet. Where shall we start?"

"Let's try to figure out what we've got so far," said Maddy pulling out her little notebook. "Have some coffee." She pointed to the carafe and a plate of fresh sourdough rolls. After about half an hour, they were getting tired and discouraged again. Andante was being a pest, taking advantage of their concentration and jumping onto the table to lick the butter knife. Penny was rambling off words hoping something would sound intelligible, when Maddy snapped to attention.

"Say that again!" "What? Oh, uh, mare something spray wheat anvil."

"Wheat anvil—Wheatonville," said Maddy. Who had been talking to her about Wheatonville lately? She stared off into space trying to bring the conversation to mind.

"I grew up in Wheatonville and graduated just before they closed the school and started busing the kids here to Marshallhaven... and I was also the last Miss Wheatonville... They hadn't had a pageant for several years and my three friends and I and our Mothers decided to put on one more pageant before the school closed."

"Oh, my goodness, it's Janet." She looked down at her notebook. "It's not 'spray', it's 'mist'. Mist Wheat Anvil. Miss Wheatonville."

Penny looked skeptical. "Janet strangled Zachariah Hendergast? I just don't see it."

"Hmmm. Me neither. No motive," said Maddy musingly. *That we know of*, she added in her mind.

"I don't think Janet would have the strength," said Penny.

"But it has to be her. There hadn't been any Miss Wheatonville's for several years previously, and she was the last," argued Maddy, "and Joe said that using a garotte wouldn't actually take as much strength as you think."

"But that's only part of the message," said Penny.

"Maybe the murderer is someone associated with Janet."

"Who? Stan? But he's a big teddy bear!" said Maddy. Then she looked back at the notebook. "Let's look again at the rest."

"Canes moth towels what fan," started Penny. "Stop!" said Maddy, "Cain! Cain was a farmer, and he was a murderer."

"OK, I think you're on to something," said Penny, "but there were definitely two canes in the picture."

"That means that the 's' is part of the next word," said Maddy. "Smoth?"

"No, wait," said Penny excitedly, "It's 'smothers'! S Moth Hers."

"But that doesn't make sense either," said Maddy. "Hendergast was strangled."

"Silly, Hendergast made this message thirty years before he was strangled. It points to the person, but a different crime. A crime worthy of some heavy duty blackmail."

Maddy smacked her forehead. "Duh!"

"Am I interrupting anything?" Kimberly stood in the doorway in her bathrobe and bunny slippers. Her eyes were sleep-blurred, but her glossy shoulder length hair was as perfect as last night.

"Oh, Kimberly, I'm so sorry if we woke you!" said Maddy jumping to her feet.

"No, I was ready to get up anyway. I just peeked in on Mark, and he's still asleep. I don't think anything could wake him right now."

"I haven't gotten any breakfast ready, except coffee for Jack. It's half-caf if you want some.

Kimberly started to move toward the kitchen. "Oh, please don't bother. I can get some for myself. You look pretty busy. Can I start making breakfast?"

Oh, she was a gem, thought Maddy. "Um, sure. I was going to make eggs and pancakes. The pancake mix is in the cupboard there and the eggs are in the fridge." Penny kicked Maddy under the table. "Oh, let me introduce you to my friend, Penny. Penny, this is Kimberly, Mark's girlfriend."

"Pleased to meet you," said Penny with a wide smile.

"Nice meeting you, too. I'll let you know when it's ready," said Kimberly with a smile and headed into the kitchen. "Wow! She's gorgeous and she cooks! When are they getting married?" asked Penny staring after her.

Maddy looked at her sideways and said, "Hopefully not too soon. Let's get back to this."

Penny looked at the next words. "What fan, who fan, why fan…"

"Wife," interjected Maddy. "Why fan—'wife and'. Cain smothers wife and… and what? And…

something…Miss Wheatonville." It became clearer like a light on a dimmer switch getting brighter and brighter. "It has to be Stan. He murdered his first wife, Claire, before he married Janet."

"But Claire died of cancer," said Penny, "I remember." She stopped. "Unless she was recovering or wasn't dying fast enough." She looked at Maddy horrified.

Maddy suddenly remembered what had bothered her on Thursday night. Stan had said that he was there to check on the lawnmower. But no one should have known about the lawnmower being left out. Jack put it away and Maddy hadn't told anyone about that part. Her story about finding Roy started with hearing the window breaking. The only way he could know about the lawnmower was if he had been there, and if he had been there and not helped Jack and Maddy rescue Roy, then he must have been the one that hit him and broke the window.

She shivered. Stan was the murderer, and he had intended to hurt Maddy on Thursday. But what had changed his mind? That was only one of the many unanswered questions that she had to find the answers to.

"We have to tell someone." She grabbed up the notebook, she stuffed it in her purse, moved toward the door and said, "Let's go tell Jack. He'll know what to do."

"Does this mean you won't be having breakfast?" asked Kimberly from the doorway.

"Oh, dear, no. We have to go out. Please enjoy some yourself and when Mark gets up…"

"Have no fear. I'll feed him when he gets up," said Kimberly, "Please, don't worry about me."

"Oh, thank you, you're a dear," said Maddy as they rushed out the door.

CHAPTER SEVENTEEN

Jack listened with a deepening frown. "You need to tell the sheriff," he said calmly.

"Oh. Right. I did tell Joe I would tell him if I found out anything more." Maddy picked up the phone and dialed his home number. It was Saturday, but she knew he wouldn't mind. When he picked up she explained what they'd found. She frowned, made a couple short answers, and then said goodbye and hung up.

"Well," said Penny impatiently. "What did he say?"

"I don't think he believed me," said Maddy. "He said there was nothing he could do because this didn't constitute proof and there was no other evidence." Jack nodded as if he'd known that would be the response.

"Well, we need to go talk to Stan and ask him," said Maddy with determination.

"We?" said Jack.

"Well, yes, you, too. I don't think you want Penny and me to go by ourselves." She smiled sheepishly.

Jack sighed. "You're right about that. Let me get my jacket. I'll drive." The three of them piled into Jack's Subaru wagon. It was old but sturdy, and it had all-wheel drive. Jack depended on it to get him out to any farm over any and all country roads in the winter. As he drove, he asked, "So, what are you going to say when we get there?"

"Um, I hadn't thought about it. I don't know. It depends." She thought in silence for a while and soon they were turning into the long driveway of the Johnsons' farm.

Janet answered the door in a mismatched sweat suit and slippers. "We're very sorry to intrude like this," said Jack politely, "but is Stan around?"

"Yes, he's in one of the outbuildings. I can call him on his cell phone. Can I tell him why you're here?"

"Maybe that should wait until he gets here," said Jack smoothly.

"Uh, sure. I'll call him then," said Janet starting to look worried. "Please come in and have a seat." They sat in the living room while Janet called Stan. "He says he'll be here in just a few minutes. Would you like something to drink?"

She got iced tea and coffee for them and they all sipped quietly until they heard Stan's footstep at the back door. He came in and immediately went to Janet and put his arm around her.

"Are you OK? You sounded upset. What's going on?" he said with concern. "I'm fine," she said and looked nervously toward their three guests.

"Pastor," he said shaking Jack's hand. "To what do I owe the pleasure of your visit?" In answer, Jack looked at Maddy questioningly.

Maddy cleared her throat. "Maybe we should all sit down." Stan looked cautious, but he slowly sat down with Janet beside him. Maddy didn't know how to begin, so she just cut to the chase.

"Stan, how did your first wife die?" The response was immediate. Stan's face went rigid, his fists clenched, his muscles bunched, and his eyes looked distant and wary. Maddy realized with alarm that this was a very large and powerful man. If he were to try to run, or to hurt any of them, the four of them would be no match for him, even with Jack on their side. The tense moment passed as quickly as it had come, and Stan sagged.

He seemed to shrink, and his eyes were full of misery as he asked huskily, "How did you find out?"

"Find out what?" demanded Janet, but Stan ignored her.

"It was the windows," answered Maddy simply.

Stan nodded. "I knew you were figuring them out. When I took your notebook, I knew you were almost there. But I didn't know what they meant. It all seemed like nonsense to me." Maddy outlined the solution to the puzzle, as much as she knew.

Stan groaned. "He told me he'd put a message in plain sight. I didn't know what he meant, didn't really believe him, until after he was dead." He paused.

"Maybe you should start at the beginning," said Jack softly.

Stan nodded, then took a deep breath. "I suppose the beginning would be with Claire. We dated all through high school. Everyone accepted us as a couple. Everyone expected us to get married. We were homecoming king and queen. And until senior year, I thought I wanted to marry her, too. But then Janet started coming to our youth group at church. Once I met her, I knew I wanted to marry Janet and not Claire. But Claire adored me. She seemed to think that we were engaged, even though I don't really remember proposing. My parents expected us to get married, too. Why, I think my mom and Claire's mother had the wedding planned since the middle of our junior year.

I didn't know what to do. I couldn't break it off with Claire. She would have been crushed, and I would have been vilified. I didn't know if Janet felt the same way about me as I felt about her, but I just wanted to be near her. I spent as much time as I could at church activities in hopes of seeing her. I don't think Claire ever realized. Our wedding day is a blur even now. I just remember Claire's radiant face gazing up at me, and then finding myself walking down the aisle with her. We were married and that was that. I could never have Janet.

I tried to love Claire. I guess I never really had. Oh sure, there was the initial crush, and then it was just comfortable to have a date, to have a girlfriend all through high school. But I never loved her the way I loved Janet. So there I was, married to Claire, and everyone thinking we were madly in love—high school sweethearts. And then Claire was diagnosed with cervical cancer. I was so happy. I'm embarrassed and ashamed to say it, but I was. I thought God was working things out for me. You know, calling Claire home to heaven and I would be free to marry Janet.

Thinking that things were going to work out for me like that, I could play the part of the concerned and grieving husband. I doted on her through the surgery and the chemotherapy. And when she had her stroke due to the chemotherapy, I was elated. This was it. She looked so bad in the hospital; I thought it couldn't be long. I called Pastor Schultz and he brought her communion and prayed with us.

But she didn't die. She started to recover. Gradually she was able to walk again with help. The doctor said there was a good chance that her cancer was in remission even though he wouldn't know for sure until the next set of clean tests. I was in despair. Now I had an invalid wife that I didn't love, and Janet was as out of reach as ever. I had started seeing her while Claire was in the hospital. Playing the depressed and overwhelmed husband that needed a shoulder to lean on. We had gotten so close and I even thought she was falling in love with me. Claire was coming home. She still took pain medication, but she didn't need it all the time anymore. She still spent most of her time in bed.

I let people think she still had her cancer and that she was dying from it. I went to the pharmacy and said that she'd lost her prescription of morphine so I could get another one. Then I dissolved about ten tablets in her soup and seasoned it well so she wouldn't taste it. I coaxed her to finish it all, saying she needed to get her strength back. But she still didn't die. Her breathing was so shallow I could hardly detect it, but her heart was still beating. So I took a pillow and held it over her face until she finally stopped breathing.

I was so shocked at what I'd done, that I just sat there for about an hour. It was about 4 a.m. I called the doctor and said that I'd gone in to check on her and she'd died in her sleep. I said I didn't know what to do, and he said he'd take care of everything. No one suspected a thing. When her doctor asked if I wanted an autopsy, I said I didn't think I could handle the idea, with everything we'd been through, and anyway, didn't we already know what she died of? He was sympathetic and just filled out the death certificate.

It was hard to take all the sympathy, but I made an outward show of being grief stricken. I cried on Janet's shoulder and spent as much time with her as I could. A few months later, I proposed, and we were married. Finally, we could be together. The church had burned down just after our wedding and the planning for rebuilding had begun. Things were looking up all around. A new life for me and a new start for the church.

And then Zachariah Hendergast told me to meet him in the park where he lived in that camper of his. I was suspicious but I went. He said he knew about Claire, how she really died. He said he had the records from the pharmacy for the extra prescription of morphine, and he'd overheard the undertaker talking to the pharmacist, saying that he'd had to use some kind of eye drops on Claire to cover up the broken blood vessels in her eyes and extra makeup around her nose, so she'd look good for the funeral. *Weren't bloodshot eyes and bruising of the nose signs of suffocation?* he'd asked me slyly.

He had me and he knew it. He told me that he wanted me to make sure he got the commission from the church for the stained-glass windows, and he wanted to be paid handsomely for it. He also hinted that Roger McBride would back me up in pushing the council to hire him.

that lots of people leave church bulletins lying around and he readily accepted that neither of us recognized Hendergast from his picture.

I thought for a time that the two 'accidental' window breakages would keep me safe, but I overheard you two talking at lunch the other day and realized that not only had you continued to find the pictures, you'd found the one from a window I'd broken and you were getting close to the solution. I had to know how much you knew. When I saw your notebook and found out how far along you were, I was crazy with desperation."

Stan's eyes drifted away from Maddy and he began speaking in a more detached tone, as if she wasn't there. "I thought of breaking another window, one she hadn't deciphered yet, and Thursday was the perfect time. Everyone went straight home from church; it was dark with no moon. I just hid in the shadow of the trees until everyone was gone. I thought the coast was clear and moved in toward the church when she suddenly appeared around the corner. I stopped in my tracks and she hesitated but continued on. I thought I had lucked out and moved back toward the trees again, when she saw me move again. I knew what I had to do. She had to be silenced. She knew too much and now she'd seen me. It was then or never. I hurried to get it over with, and then she tripped and fell. Just as I raised my hand to hit her, she turned. I will never forget the terror on her face. In that look I saw what I had become—a monster. I had killed twice and bludgeoned a third into unconsciousness, and now I was going to kill again, and it seemed so easy. Easy to decide to do it, easy to have carried it out. Except for that look. What had she done to deserve death? Nothing. She hadn't tricked anyone into marrying her. She hadn't blackmailed anyone. She'd just been curious. I couldn't do it. I didn't know what I was going to do, but I couldn't hurt her. And then after I helped her up, I realized she hadn't recognized me before. She believed my lie about checking on the lawn mower. She wasn't faking; I could see the relief in her face. I had a little more time.

I had to think about things, what I would do if and when you finally solved it. I knew that it was only a matter of time until the truth came out, and I realized that I couldn't continue hurting people who got close to the truth. The truth was going to come out anyway, and I couldn't live with the monster I had become. I thought about going into hiding. Just disappearing. People did that sometimes, starting new lives with new names. But what about Janet? I thought about faking my death and leaving the farm to Brian and taking Janet with me. But I didn't know what she would say when she knew the truth or if she would come with me. I even thought of taking my own life. I thought it would be justice. I could leave a note explaining everything. But I just couldn't do that to Janet and the boys. Then you showed up this morning and I knew it was too late.

In a way, I'm relieved. I've been hiding this for thirty years, and I'm tired. I am sorry about Roy. I didn't mean to hit him that hard. I kept thinking that he would leave, but the storm was getting worse and he just kept tinkering around. Then, for whatever reason, he left the lawn mower and came around the corner of the church right toward me. I guess he was checking on the repair to the previous broken window, because of the storm, but I couldn't let him see me. I'm glad he's going to be OK."

He stopped speaking and the silence hung heavily. During the narration, Janet had shrunk away from him on the loveseat as if he were diseased. He looked at her and there was deep sadness in his eyes.

"Janet, can you ever forgive me?"

Janet's eyes were blank and lifeless. "I... I don't know," she said in a monotone.

Stan turned to Jack. "Can God forgive me?"

Jack nodded. "Come into the other room with me. But first I think you need to make a call." Stan looked confused for a moment, but quickly realized what Jack meant.

He reached for the phone and dialed. "Hello? Joe?" He paused, took a deep breath, and then continued without preamble. "I killed Zachariah Hendergast and also my first wife, Claire Johnson." Pause. "Yes. Pastor and his wife are here. I'll stay here with them until you get here." He hung up and then moved toward the other room with Jack following.

Although Maddy couldn't hear through the closed door, in her mind she heard the familiar words of the pastor offering absolution, 'Do you believe that the forgiveness that you are about to receive is from God Himself…?' She turned to Janet, who still looked like a zombie.

Janet said lifelessly, "What am I going to do? My whole life has just been destroyed. Everything I thought was true has turned out to be hideously false. I'm repulsed by him now, yet I still love him." Tears started running down her cheeks, but her eyes were still dead.

Maddy put a comforting arm around her, but it was like hugging a statue. "Well, the first thing you are going to do is call your lawyer. Then you're going to call Brian and your other sons and let them know what's happened. I'll take you to the sheriff's office, and Brian can meet you there and bring you home. Then you are going to visit Stan in prison as often as it is allowed. You'll probably want to talk to Pastor about all of this, too." She nodded. She was becoming slightly less wooden, but her lifeless eyes still worried Maddy. "And you'll need to rely on your friends for support," finished Maddy. She suddenly thought about Janet's life on the farm, surrounded by her husband and children, with Brian and his fiancé building their home here, too, miles from town, busy with farm chores—she probably didn't have a lot of friends.

"You know, Penny and I meet for lunch every Tuesday. Would you like to join us?"

Finally, Janet's eyes showed signs of life. She nodded and a tentative but hopeful look came into her face. "Yes," she said, "I'd like that."

CHAPTER EIGHTEEN

The phone rang at 3:42 a.m. *Who could be calling this late?* thought Maddy wearily. Or rather *'this early'?* They'd only been asleep for a few hours. Easter Vigil had ended around 11 p.m. and she had then gotten everything ready for the Easter Sunrise Service, which would begin around 6 a.m. She hoped it wasn't an emergency that required Jack to go out.

Jack was saying into the phone, "I'll tell her. You take care of her and try to get a little sleep." He hung up and turned to Maddy with a broad smile.

"That was Harlan. Martha went into labor right in the middle of Easter Vigil, so the elders finished the service while he bundled her into the car and took her to the emergency room without even bothering to change out of his robes, which apparently provided some amusement for the emergency room staff and patients. She just delivered a healthy little girl—our new granddaughter Alice Marie. Eight pounds, two ounces."

Maddy sank back onto her pillows with a sigh of utter delight. A little girl! Oh, how she would spoil her rotten! Jack started getting up and Maddy realized that the alarm was about to go off anyway. She got ready in a pleasant haze, nearly forgetting yesterday's drama. She went to wake up Mark and Kimberly, and to give Mark the news of his new niece.

Halfway through her shower, she realized that Joanna didn't know the good news. She towel-dried her hair, then grabbed the phone by the bed.

"Joanna? I'm so glad I caught you. Martha had her baby! A little girl, your first niece. They named her Alice Marie." Maddy continued with the saga of Harlan rushing her to the hospital in his robes, which got a good laugh from Joanna.

"Oh, Mom, that's wonderful!" she said finally. "You just caught me. Seamus is supposed to be picking me up any minute now. And I've been talking to him and he's agreed to 'try out the church thing' with me. I had to agree to go to the cathedral for

Easter instead of the Hope Lutheran where I go, but he finally saw how important it is to me and will come with me on Sundays. I hope you have a wonderful Easter! Love you!" and she hung up.

Maddy set the phone back in its cradle and sighed. The last weight had just lifted from her heart. The murderer had been caught, the river was receding, Martha had her baby and both were healthy, Holy Week was over, and Joanna's boyfriend would be going to church with her. Maybe he would turn out to be a good boyfriend for Joanna and perhaps a good husband in the future. An artist, hmmm? She'd been both intrigued with Zachariah Hendergast's art and repelled by his lifestyle. She would be interested to see some of Seamus's art.

Maddy shook herself and turned her thoughts back to getting her family and herself ready and out the door in time for the sunrise service. Mark looked dazed, whether from the news of his new niece or from lack of sleep, Maddy wasn't sure. Kimberly looked like she'd just spent an hour getting ready even though Maddy knew it had only been about twenty minutes. Her hair was perfect, her eyes bright. She was wearing a stunning white sleeveless dress with rose embroidery around the hem and arm openings that showed up beautifully next to her dark, creamy skin. She was pouring coffee for Jack and Mark and had made toast to tide everyone over until the Easter breakfast between services. Could anyone really be this perfect? She gratefully grabbed a piece of toast, being careful not to get crumbs on her own dress, a green rayon wraparound that swirled delightfully when she walked.

Sunrise service was over before she knew it and everyone was heading toward the parish hall for Easter breakfast, compliments of the youth group.

Mark, who had been thrilled with the news of Alice's arrival, had headed immediately to the church kitchen to greet his high school friends. "Hey, Everyone! Guess What? I'm an Uncle!" he had announced, and between that and introducing Kimberly, became an instant celebrity.

Out in the parish hall, around the various tables, the conversation buzzed with a different topic. Stan's arrest had happened around 9 a.m. yesterday, so there was time for word to get around. After taking Janet down to the Sheriff's office and driving home, Maddy and Penny had looked again at the rebus and the windows. Knowing what to look for, they had quickly found the picture of the eels in the window depicting the Temptation of Adam and Eve. They'd known they were eels and not snakes because of the little lightning bolts coming from them. That gave a complete sequence of "Canes Moth Hers Why Fan Mare Eels Mist Wheat Anvil" or "Cain smothers wife and marries Miss Wheatonville". They had laughed a bit at the liberties Zachariah had taken with 'eels' and 'mist'. It wasn't the best puzzle she'd ever seen, yet it had done its job and led them to Stan.

Although everyone knew the basic details, they wanted fresh details about Maddy's role in deciphering the windows and they crowded around her for information. She gave as much detail as she thought was prudent but withheld anything she thought too personal to Janet or the rest of the family.

Mostly satisfied, everyone turned to other topics. Something had bothered her during the retelling. She looked around and saw Roger sitting by himself a table away. She got up and sat next to him.

"This must be uncomfortable for you. It's bound to bring up some painful memories," she said to him sympathetically.

He looked at her for a moment and then nodded. "Yep," he said laconically.

"Do you mind if I ask you a question?" He nodded wordlessly. Maddy continued, "Stan said that you both were being blackmailed to support his bid for the stained-glass windows, but if you agreed to Zachariah Hendergast's demands, why did he tell your wife?"

Roger stared at the table a moment and then looked up at Maddy. "He didn't. I panicked when he told me what he knew. I agreed to do what he wanted, but I thought that if he figured it out, someone else might, too. I tried to go back and cover my tracks. It was my efforts to hide things that actually tipped her off. Funny, huh? I blamed him at first, but it wasn't long until I admitted that it was my owned dam.. uh.. darn..., uh, my own fault." He looked at her sheepishly.

Maddy nodded and smiled gently. "Thanks. I didn't mean to pry, but I just wondered."

"It's alright. It was a long time ago, and I've made my peace with God and my neighbors, if not my ex-wife. Not that I didn't try."

Maddy nodded again and then tactfully changed the topic. She told Roger about their new granddaughter. Soon he was smiling.

"Congratulations! That's just great. If you'll excuse me now, I think I'll get me some more coffee." Roger got up and moved toward the large coffee urns and Maddy started clearing tables.

"Oh, you don't have to do that! We're doing everything," said a perky teenager who was pushing a dish cart. Maddy smiled and placed the dishes on the cart. "I heard that Martha had her baby! That's cool! Is it a boy or a girl? What did they name it?"

"A girl, Alice Marie," answered Maddy. Basking in her happy glow, she headed back toward the church for the ten o'clock service.

Janet was standing in the narthex, talking to one of her sons. It looked like Ian, though Ian and Fred looked so similar, that since they'd gone off to college, Maddy had trouble telling them apart when they came home for holidays.

"...still can't believe it," Ian was saying. He put his arm around his mother. "I still think you need us at home."

"No! Absolutely not! You and Fred are going to finish college." Janet's voice was forceful and commanding. "Brian can handle the farm just fine, and we'll hire any extra help we need. You will not throw away your future just because your father is serving his sentence."

Maddy was happy to see the fire in Janet's eyes. It was a vast improvement over the cold deadness of yesterday. Janet turned and saw Maddy and smiled, but there was still a hardness in her eyes. Time would soften them, but for now, she needed strength.

"Hi! I'm glad to see that Ian and Fred made it home so soon," she said, realizing too late that they had probably planned to come home for Easter anyway.

"Yes, and can you believe that the first thing they said was that they were going to quit school and come home? Like it would help things for them to become minimum wage earners instead of college graduates!" She rolled her eyes in mock disbelief. It seemed she was regaining her sense of humor, too.

Ian grinned sheepishly and moved off to join his brothers' conversation behind them.

"How are you really doing?" asked Maddy more quietly.

"I'm coping," said Janet succinctly. "There's so much to arrange." She stopped and looked Maddy in the eye. "But that's not what you meant was it?"

Maddy shook her head. Janet had experienced worse than Maddy's worst nightmare. Janet's eyes unfocused a little as she answered.

"I have a lot to work through. I've lost my husband, and not just because he went to prison. I've lost the man I married and lived with for thirty years. Sometimes I'm not sure if that man ever existed. And now I have a husband who is a murderer, yet repentant. I know him, yet I don't know him. I think I will be getting to know him all over again, and hopefully I will fall in love with him again. If not, then I pray that God will give me the strength to at least forgive him and love him anyway for the sake of our children and for my sanity." She smiled sadly.

Maddy was astounded. Janet had wells of strength and character that Maddy was pretty sure she didn't have herself. At a loss for words, she simply took Janet into a hug. Janet's firmly returned hug told Maddy of the need behind the strength. She reiterated her promise of support. Janet looked at her fiercely and smiled again. "Thank you. I'll be needing it."

Maddy was still a little early for service, but she wanted to just sit and think a little. Finding the murderer hadn't brought joy and relief to everyone. It was painful to Stan's family and friends to find out the truth about him. As one of Stan's friends, Maddy was feeling that pain, too. But it was better to know the truth, however painful. That was what she was seeing in Janet. Better the bitter truth than the comfortable falsehood. Maddy let her eyes wander around the church.

The volunteers had outdone themselves. Over fifty donated white Easter lilies spilled over the chancel steps and dipped gently over several stands placed around the sanctuary. Two white banners with gold lettering hung at each side of the chancel. One, decorated with lilies and trumpets proclaimed, "He is Risen!" The other showed the empty tomb with the abandoned grave cloths and said, "See Where They Laid Him." The crucifix was covered in a white veil, the only day of the year that the corpus was not visible, emphasizing that the crucified Savior is alive. The white paraments on the altar were embroidered with the Lamb bleeding from a wound on his chest and holding a banner in the crook of his leg. The paraments on the pulpit and lectern featured a crown and a four-pointed star in the shape of a cross. Babs had outdone herself with huge, gorgeous altar arrangements of lilies, white roses, dogwood and white chrysanthemums with sprays of baby's breath and green fronds. The sun, having cooperated beautifully and rising right on time for the beginning of the sunrise service, was now shining in through the windows, casting a kaleidoscope of color over the white trimmings. Maddy sat, absorbing the overwhelming symbols of atonement and thought of Stan.

Stan had made a full confession in the presence of his lawyer and signed it at the time of his booking. His lawyer had then contacted the judge, and, after a brief consultation with Stan, announced that he intended to plead guilty in return for a twenty-year sentence with the possibility of parole in ten years. Stan seemed almost eager to begin serving his sentence, to pay his debt, as he'd put it. Twenty years didn't really seem long enough for two murders, one of them premeditated. But it was what the legal system had agreed on as a just punishment, and they apparently felt that his full confession and the involvement of his pastor suggested internal reform and a low chance of recidivism should he be paroled when the time came. Certainly, the plea bargain would spare Janet and the family a trial. Of course, this was all in the civil realm, the kingdom of the law. In the church, the kingdom of grace, Stan was fully forgiven.

Joe had bawled her out for going out to the farm without telling him, and didn't she know how dangerous that had been? But she reminded him that she *had* called him, and she explained that she thought it was the only way to get any real answers, and it wasn't like she was alone—Jack and Penny had been with her. He hadn't been very happy about it but didn't know what else to say. He and Jack had talked a bit, with Jack remarking that Joe's job was done, but his, Jack's, was just beginning. It was unknown what prison Stan would eventually be transferred to, but Jack had promised to visit at least monthly.

The organist was playing a medley of Easter hymns and Maddy listened contentedly. Her thoughts turned to their new grandbaby. She fully expected that she would soon be seeing Martha, Harlan, and little Alice at her baptism.

Soon people were filing in and filling the pews. It was going to be crowded, more so than the sunrise service. She left spaces for Mark and Kimberly, who had gone back to the house after eating a quick breakfast to pack up a little so they could spend as much time as possible with them over dinner. She also left a space on her other side—just in case. She was beginning to doubt that Sarah would really come.

She smiled and greeted people as they filled the pews around her. She smiled at Janet who was headed to a pew on the other side of the church with her assembled brood. Janet smiled back with a little knowing nod. Jack would be taking communion to Stan at the jail right after the service. Roger sat behind her and gave her a nod and a smile.

Harold stood hesitantly at the back of the nave, as if deciding where to sit. Maddy smiled broadly and waved. He looked startled, raised his hand, but glowered. He turned back to the narthex as if to leave but saw Jack approaching. His eyes fell to the floor and he hurriedly sat in the back pew. What was that Bible verse about being kind to your enemies thereby heaping burning coals on their heads? Yep, burning coals, alright.

Penny sat in the pew in front of her with her father, George, and there was Laura and Ronald. Maddy was happy to see that Ronald seemed to be having one of his better days, as they stopped to wish her a blessed Easter. He even remembered her name today. Roy came in with his wife and sat down. He looked good, despite his wife fussing over him. Without the little bandage on the back of his head where he'd had a few stitches, one would never know he'd been knocked unconscious and left for dead.

Mark and Kimberly hurriedly sat down looking very happy. Maddy suspected they had taken advantage of a few minutes alone to have a little closeness. She liked Kimberly and hoped this was the beginning of something more permanent. She even saw Lenny slip into the back pew and give her a wink as she looked to the back of the church where Jack was waiting with the crucifer and the acolytes. Jack gave her a wide smile as she blew him a little kiss.

The music swelled, signaling the start of the first hymn. A trumpet player in the choir loft began playing along with the first verse. She glanced up but couldn't tell who it was. A young man, maybe college age—a visiting family member who volunteered at the last minute? The music was rich and full and made the roots of Maddy's hair tingle with emotion. The congregation rose, turned toward the processional cross and began singing "Jesus Christ is Risen Today." Maddy bowed slightly as the crucifer passed by and as she did so, she sensed rather than saw someone take the space next to her. As she turned toward the front of the church, she saw Sarah standing next to her, determinedly focused on the service and not meeting her eye, looking for all the world like she'd been doing this every Sunday for the last thirty years. As she sang, Maddy reflected that she had wanted to solve the murder so that things could return to the way they had been. But they hadn't. They were better.

THE END

Thank you for reading *Blood Stained*.
I hope that you have enjoyed it.

Madalyn Mitchell will return in *Blood Meal*

ABOUT THE AUTHOR

Gayl Siegel is the wife of a retired Lutheran pastor. She lives in central Iowa with her husband, daughter, and two cats.

ABOUT THE ILLUSTRATOR

Kristina Helfert is a freelance artist. She lives in central Iowa with her husband, son and cat.

Blood Stained

Made in the USA
Columbia, SC
12 February 2023